# SUMMER
# BEGINS

# SUMMER BEGINS

## Sandy Asher

LODESTAR BOOKS
*E. P. Dutton   New York*

Library of Congress Cataloging in Publication Data

Asher, Sandy Fenichel.
Summer begins.
SUMMARY: the controversy she creates at school,
her mother's strange behavior, and her
sudden friendship with her best
friend's secret love leaves 13-year-old Summer
in a state of confusion.
[1. School stories. 2. Mothers and daughters—
Fiction. 3. Friendship—Fiction] I. Title.
PZ7.A816Su [Fic]          80–12321
ISBN 0–525–66696–6

Published in the United States by E. P. Dutton, Inc.,
2 Park Avenue, New York, N.Y. 10016
Published simultaneously in Ontario by Clark,
Irwin & Company Limited, Toronto and Vancouver.

Printed in the U.S.A.
10   9   8   7   6   5   4   3   2

*For MARTY and JUDY*

*The author gratefully acknowledges the support of the writing of this book by a Creative Writing Fellowship grant made by the National Endowment for the Arts.*

# SUMMER
# BEGINS

# 1

If Terry Morris had never seen the movie *All the President's Men*, things would have been very different. Or, if he had seen the movie but hadn't come out worshiping the reporters, Woodward and Bernstein, things still would have been very different. I suppose I could blame the whole mess on ex-President Nixon, but that may be farfetched. I should probably blame it all on Terry. But he's one of my best friends, and I only have two. Besides, agony that it was, it did turn out for the best.

The whole thing started when our eighth-grade home-room, Mrs. Morton's class, decided we weren't getting enough attention. I personally have never been crazy about attention. I tend to blush and get very squirmy. But it was the end of November, that weird waiting time between Thanksgiving and Christmas, and everybody was restless.

"Mrs. Morton," Marjory Warren began, in that ever-so-elegant manner of hers, "in other schools, the eighth graders are the leaders. The big shots. But here, we're nobody. Nothing. We have to wait four more years to get to the top."

Marjory has always been deeply concerned with getting to the top. Her father was a state senator once, and the family has never gotten over the thrill of it.

"Yeah," Murray Hamm put in, for once not comment-ing about someone's body, "we have to practice the same old carols for a solid month, and the seniors get to put on whatever play they choose."

Murray has a speech problem: his *s*'s are all wet. Maybe it's because of his braces. Whatever the reason, it's not hygienic. He sits behind me in homeroom and I am thankful that my hair covers my neck.

This was a rare occasion: I had to agree with Murray and Marjory. We go to University School, which belongs to Middletown University. University School goes from kindergarten straight through high school. The two other schools in town stop at sixth grade or eighth grade. Then everybody goes either to Washington Junior High or directly into Roxbury High. Either way, as Marjory said,

10

eighth graders get to be the big shots. Until they go to Roxbury High, anyway.

"Well, what would you like to do about it?" Mrs. Morton asked, poking her glasses back up her nose. Mrs. Morton is really nice. Everybody thinks so. Except a couple of boys, Soggy Hamm, for instance, who make fun of her because she wears thick glasses and has buckteeth. I'll admit that when you first look at her, it's not too pleasant a sight. But once you get to know her, she seems to get prettier. I wish I knew how she manages that, because I wear kind of thick glasses myself. I don't have buckteeth, though.

My best friend, Reggie Wilson, raised her hand. "Let's put on a play, too," she said. "Let's just go ahead and do it. And then we'll all get discovered by talent scouts and become famous. That'll show 'em."

There were moans and groans around the room.

"A play?" Mrs. Morton echoed. "I don't know, Reggie. Homeroom is only twenty minutes. When could we rehearse?"

Reggie shrugged her shoulders and giggled. She has these amazing ideas all the time and no way to get them done. It never bothers her. Once she suggested we all—the entire class—run away to Paris. Run away to Paris, can you believe that? What were we supposed to do, hijack a troop carrier?

Terry Morris was talking. "We could start a newspaper," he said. There were several titters in response to that. Ever since that movie, Terry has been trying to start a newspaper. "We could organize it together in class, but

11

work on it separately at home. Or anywhere. That way it wouldn't take up much school time. The press is very powerful. Nobody can ignore a newspaper."

There is an old saying about an idea whose time has come. Well, Terry's newspaper's time, at long last, had come. The titters stopped.

"Let's do it," Paul DuBerry yelled. "I want to write about sports."

Then everyone was roaring at once.

"Oh, wow, entertainment," Beverly Simmons screeched.

"A comic strip!"

"Crossword puzzles!"

"State news!" (That was Marjory Warren, of course, the well-known ex-senator's daughter.)

"Gossip column!" Reggie squealed, bouncing on her seat beside me. "Oh, please, please, please, Mrs. Morton, let me write the gossip column. Oh, please, oh, please, oh, pleee-eeeese."

Mrs. Morton, who is, after all, an English teacher, grinned so wide that her eyeglasses slipped down to the tip of her nose. (Her nose is incredibly small, by the way, especially compared to her teeth.)

Well, that's how the *Eighth Grade Reporter* was born. Terry was named editor in chief, naturally. Blushing like a pumpkin to the roots of his funny yellow hair, he gave this very amusing pep talk after his election. He promised that whoever got a really big scoop and rocked the entire school would get a raise.

Mrs. Morton laughed. "I don't know about the raise,"

she said, "but I will make it an assignment for English class that everyone must contribute something to the newspaper. And I'll give extra credit to those who do an especially fine job."

"What are you going to write about?" Reggie asked as we jostled our way up the hall toward math class.

"I don't know," I moaned. "I think I'm going to hate this assignment."

"Summer Smith!" Reggie squawked. "English is your favorite subject. You love to write."

"I love to write and show it to you or Mrs. Morton or nobody. I don't love to write and show it to the whole school."

"Oh, you're just being silly. Why don't you write an editorial? That's easy. You just give your opinion about something."

But I didn't have opinions. I made a special point never to have opinions. I found that kept me out of trouble about 99.9 percent of the time. I've never liked trouble. I'd gladly cross the street to stay out of its way. I never grumbled about teachers, clothes, curfews, tests, reports, cars, where we took our vacation, what we watched on TV. I never gossiped to anyone, except Reggie. And sometimes Terry. Terry and Reggie are my best friends, but I have no enemies. I would die if I had enemies. I couldn't stand it.

"Write about the Christmas program," Reggie went on. "Tell them how we don't think it's fair that seniors get to do whatever they want and we have to sing carols with the elementary kids every year. Do you realize we've been doing the exact same program for nine straight years?"

"Reggie, the Christmas program is a *tradition*. They've been doing the exact same program, with us or without us, for about a thousand years. They don't care what *we* think about it. Besides, it gives you something to look forward to when you're a senior."

"I guess. Hey, did you know I'm going to do a gossip column?"

"Of course, I know. I was right there when Mrs. Morton appointed you."

"Oh, yeah. How did she know I wanted it so badly?" Reggie wondered. "She's terrific, isn't she? She always knows these things. Maybe she reads minds."

"She knew because you practically jumped into her lap when she asked for volunteers," I said. Reggie's a good, true friend, but she's a little scatterbrained.

"Oh, yeah," she said, and giggled. "But she's still the greatest teacher in the world." Reggie can laugh at herself. That's one of my favorite things about her. Nothing much bothers her. She just giggles it away.

"Ooooooooo," she squealed suddenly. Her eyes practically fell out of her head. Then she skittered sideways into the ladies' room. I recognized the symptoms. It took me about a second and a half to locate Rod Whitman. There he was, sauntering down the hall toward us. In no time at all, Reggie was back beside me, fresh lipstick on her best sexy smile. Only she also had fresh lipstick on her front teeth.

"Reggie, there's lipstick on your teeth," I hissed. Her mouth clamped shut just as Rod glanced our way. Poor

Reggie looked like someone trying not to sneeze. Very sexy. Rod kind of half-smiled in our direction and continued down the hall.

"Oh, my God, he's so gorgeous," Reggie gasped.

Actually, Rod was half-smiling at me, I think. We're neighbors. He lives right around the corner from me. Sometimes I think that has a lot to do with why Reggie Wilson is my best friend. She's been in love with Rod since kindergarten. (She was a very early bloomer.) Rod was in fourth grade then; he's a senior, now. Basketball captain, senior-class president, all-around Greek god. Reggie carries on as if she had played a part in making him what he is today. Well, she did pick him for a winner eight years ago, you have to give her that.

All these years, she's been coming over to my house practically every day and begging me to play outside. Even in the rain. Even when it's ten below zero. Maybe six times in the last eight years, Rod has wandered by while we were out there playing or freezing or whatever. We got the same half-smile every time. I also get it when I pass him alone, so I have this sneaky feeling he still doesn't know Reggie exists. Of course, I'd never tell her that.

"Oh, my God, he's so gorgeous," she said again. She pulled a tissue out of her purse and wiped the lipstick off her teeth. "How can you stand to live right around the corner from him, Summer? I don't know how you stand it."

Reggie always says that. But she knows very well it's not that big a deal.

Suddenly, she gasped, stopped short and dug her four

15

good nails into my arm. (She's giving up nail-biting, one finger a month.)

"Ow! What are you doing?"

"Don't turn around now," she muttered between clenched teeth, "but tell me, did he meet Cindy Grant?"

Involuntarily, my head started to turn.

"I said don't turn around," Reggie hissed, squeezing harder.

"If you draw blood, Reggie," I told her, as calmly as I could, considering the pain, "I will march right up to Rod Whitman and tell him you love him."

Reggie dropped my arm as if it'd turned into a snake. "You wouldn't do that, Summer," she said.

"Of course not. I only said it in self-defense."

"Oh. Well, is he with Cindy?"

"I'll have to look. I can't tell you if I don't look."

"Well, okay. But don't make it obvious."

"Okay." While I slowly turned around, Reggie made herself totally inconspicuous by staring at the ceiling and whistling "Deck the Halls with Boughs of Holly." Rod was standing outside biology lab at the end of the hall. With Cindy Grant. I had to report the news as I saw it.

"Oh, my God," Reggie whimpered. "Is she wearing her cheerleading outfit?"

She was.

"Is he holding her hand?"

He was.

"Ooooo! Good-bye, Summer. I'm going to kill myself."

"Let's go to math," I suggested. "It amounts to the same thing."

16

We were quiet the rest of the way to math class. We were at the door before I realized just how quiet we were. I looked at Reggie. Tears trickled down her cheeks.

"Oh, Reggie, don't suffer over him. Please don't. There are lots of other guys."

"Not like him."

"Well, that's true."

"I hate Cindy Grant's guts."

"Okay, if you want to. But it won't do any good." I sounded calm and sensible, but inside I was wincing. I don't like people to hate each other. I don't like the word "hate." It makes me nervous.

Reggie pulled yet another tissue out of her purse and wiped her eyes. I said she could laugh off almost everything. The exception, unfortunately, is Love. She probably keeps the Kleenex company in business, poor kid. Thank goodness, I'm not in love with anybody.

Math, science, Spanish, lunch, English, history, and home. They were all one big blur. I got to thinking about that newspaper article. It bugged me until I couldn't think about anything else. Not that I had a topic to consider. That was the problem. I kept thinking that I didn't have anything to think about. Then I got to thinking about someone thinking about not having anything to think about. And then I got to thinking about other people thinking about someone who was thinking about thinking about not having anything to think about.

I had to find a topic or go crazy.

First of all, if I didn't (find a topic—not go crazy), Mrs. Morton would really be disappointed in me. And that would kill me. And second of all, by the time a person reaches eighth grade, she really ought to have an opinion about *something*. But it had to be something that wouldn't make anybody angry at me, because that would kill me, too. Either way, it wasn't a very healthy situation.

# 2

After school, Reggie and I took a bag of pretzels and mugs of milk up to the guest room in my house. Reggie likes the guest room better than my room because it used to belong to my brother, Douglas. He's at Stanford, now, in California, getting his Ph.D. He's been away at school for six years, counting college, his Master's degree, and this one. Ever since I was seven, I've only seen him summers and holidays. Considering that he's one of my favorite people in the world, that's not my idea of a terrific setup.

Anyway, Reggie is in love with Douglas, too. A lot of people would say that's impossible, but it isn't. Reggie's living proof that you can love two people at once. She was in love with Douglas even before she noticed Rod. I told you she was an early bloomer. It's her nature, I guess. Passionate genes. She was the first kid we knew to get her period and wear a bra. We were only in fifth grade! I'm a late bloomer, I guess, and that's all I care to say about that.

"What do you hear from Douglas?" Reggie asked, trying hard to sound nonchalant. She was sitting cross-legged on the other twin bed with one of my mother's scrapbooks on her lap. That's all there is to look at in the guest room, three huge scrapbooks. You really get to know exactly whose guest you are.

"Not much," I said. "He's writing his dissertation, so he doesn't write letters anymore."

"His dissertation. Wow!" Reggie sighed. "A Ph.D. Dr. Douglas Gregory Smith."

She was quiet for a minute, but I knew what she was thinking. "Dr. and Mrs. Douglas Gregory Smith."

"It must be weird to have a brother who's ten years older than you."

"Yeah, it is. It's more like having an uncle."

Reggie focused in on one of the pictures in the scrapbook. "Hey, is this you?"

I put my milk and pretzel on the night table and bounced over to her bed. The picture showed a baby swimming underwater with a woman's face, also underwater, grinning at him.

20

"No, that's Douglas." The whole scrapbook contained stuff from before I was born. In fact, all three did.

"You know," Reggie said, slowly, fingering a pimple on her chin, "you could have been an abortion."

"What?"

"If they were legal then, I bet your mother wouldn't have had you."

My mouth fell open. I jumped off the bed and ran out of the room, slamming the door behind me. "And I bet yours wouldn't have had you either," I yelled.

Reggie came right after me. "I didn't mean to hurt your feelings," she whined. "I just meant that most people don't have their kids ten years apart on purpose."

I kept my back turned on Reggie while I blew my nose. "I guess not," I said. Then, to change the subject because I can't stand unpleasantness, I added, "Well, it's about four thirty."

"It is?" Reggie shrieked. She ran downstairs ahead of me and started whipping her things together as if she had a plane to catch. Then she stood at the front window. Well, not exactly *at* it. More to the side, with one eye peering around the draperies toward school. This was Reggie's basketball-season routine. She went through it almost every day, if my parents weren't home. You see, Rod has basketball practice after school from two thirty to four. About four thirty or a quarter to five, he passes my house on his way home.

"Here he comes!" Reggie squealed. She pulled on her hat and gloves and opened the front door. "See you, Summer!" she said, very loudly.

"See you, Reggie," I said.

"Louder!" she hissed.

"See you, Reggie," I yelled.

Reggie scurried down the steps just in time to cross in front of Rod.

"Hi, Rod," she chirped.

"Hi," Rod said and kept on walking. Undaunted, Reggie threw me a wink and a wave and pranced toward home.

It would be another hour until my parents got back. They both teach at the University. I went upstairs and gathered up the pretzels and milk. The scrapbook still lay open on Douglas' old bed. I sat down and flipped through it.

Would I have been an abortion? Maybe so. Except for two things, I decided immediately. (I wanted to think one was my father and one was my mother, but I wasn't sure about that.) No, the first thing was that abortions weren't legal then. And the second, even more important thing was that when you're "America's Mermaid," you can't chance a scandal like that.

America's Mermaid. That's my mother. Maybe you don't remember, but a lot of people do. Angela Gregory, three gold medals in swimming, Summer Olympics, London, 1948. Went to Helsinki four years later, as Angela Gregory Smith, my father's beautiful bride, and took two golds in diving. Yes, fans, an athletic first.

Take that picture of Douglas swimming underwater. That's Mother with the grin, cheering him on. It's not your typical family photograph. It was clipped out of

*National Magazine*. It seems that for years every time my mother got near water, cameras surfaced like periscopes. Here's Mother giving the Atlantic Ocean her big-toe test at Coney Island. There's Mother approving of the Pacific Ocean off Big Sur. Captured by *The New York Times* and *The San Francisco Examiner*, respectively.

You know those TV commercials about the California girl? Well, they must have been thinking about Mother. Straight blond hair with natural platinum streaks, wide blue eyes, just enough freckles to be cute, tall, graceful, good at all sports. Even now, she looks as if she were outdoors even when she's not.

I don't look anything like her. I'm Daddy's Little Girl: a pale-faced string bean with glasses.

Very few of these photographs feature my father. At first, you can see that the photographers tried. After all, it was big news: America's Mermaid marries Literary Giant. That was the title on one article, really. Dad is chairman of the English Department at Middletown U. He's published seven books and he also writes critical reviews for the *American Review of Literature*. Very important, if you're big on analyzing T. S. Eliot's left big toenail. That's what Dad always tells me he's writing when I ask him. "Oh, just analyzing T. S. Eliot's left big toenail."

Anyway, I guess the photographers got really excited when the engagement was announced. They started snapping away and kept it up for the next two years; until Douglas was about eight months old. Then they gave up on Dad. I think it was because he never smiled for them. Or waved. Or anything. In every picture, he's just standing there, scowling. Actually, he's not scowling, but he looks as if he were. That's his natural expression when he's out in the sun. It doesn't make for a fascinating photograph. I mean, here's little Douglas going for his first jump off the diving board. Mother is below him, flashing up her golden grin. And there's Dad, on the board, looking as if he'd caught both of them trespassing in his pool. (We don't really have our own pool. This was taken in Florida.)

Dad isn't really a grouch. He just doesn't smile much. To tell you the truth, he's kind of shy. Mother smiles a lot, enough for both of them. Not that she's so happy. I guess she's just used to it. According to these scrapbooks, she had to smile almost constantly for about six straight years. Right up until she started coaching swimmers and divers at Middletown U. About then, the next Olympics came along, with the next bunch of medalists, and I guess the cameras disappeared. At least, that's where the scrapbooks end. But Mother goes on smiling, out of habit, I suppose. Or maybe because she's hoping the cameras will come back. Or maybe because she hasn't noticed that they're gone.

There aren't any pictures of me learning to swim. I did that at the Y, with Reggie. I passed my lifesaver's test a couple of years ago, or about twenty-three years after Mother won her second set of medals. Not exactly a major newsbreak.

Oh, wait. There is one little article about me in the last scrapbook. It's not pasted in, just wedged between two pages. It says, "Angela Gregory Smith, formerly known as

'America's Mermaid,' and her husband, literary critic Douglas Marshall Smith, announce the birth of their second child, a daughter." That's it. Not even a name.

Maybe I *would* have been an abortion. I looked up from the article and noticed the walls were kind of blurred. I wished Douglas were home. He'd know how things were when I was born. After all, he was ten years old. In spite of the achy feeling in my throat, I suddenly found myself smiling. I was thinking about Douglas and those walls, those gold-and-brown he-man walls my mother had insisted on even though Douglas wanted sky blue. "Me, Tarzan; you, Jane," he used to grunt, teasing her. Then he'd lope around the house with one hand dangling to the ground and the other scratching his armpit. He'd make this crazy ape face and chatter like a chimpanzee. I'd laugh so hard I'd get the hiccups. Reggie was there once and wet her pants.

I really miss Douglas. He's never mean like other brothers. He really brightens a place up. A California boy, even though he was born in the Midwest, like me. Douglas would never have been an abortion.

I thought about writing an editorial about abortions. Maybe I could look up all kinds of famous people who were born when their parents were pretty old, like mine. People who really did the world a lot of good. How old was Einstein's mother? I wondered.

No, they'd never let me write about abortions. Too controversial. Even if they did, everybody would be on my back about it. And I couldn't stand that. I needed a nice quiet topic.

Besides, there are probably a lot of late kids who grew up to be mass murderers, too. And even more who turned out kind of like me. Nothing special.

# 3

On Monday, December 5, we arrived in homeroom to find this schedule on the board:

Monday, Dec. 12
   deadline for newspaper articles. ABSOLUTELY NO EXCUSES. [The last three words were underlined twice.]
Monday, Dec. 12
   through Friday, December 16
   edit articles, type and run off stencils, collate papers.
Monday, Dec. 19
   distribute newspapers to other classrooms.

Friday, Dec. 23
distribute extra copies to guests at Christmas program.

Editors, please come to a brief meeting today after school.
Terry Morris, Editor in Chief
Virginia Morton, Publisher


"Isn't that neat?" Reggie said, after reading the message.

"No," I moaned. "I don't even have a topic yet, let alone a finished article."

"I mean the way Mrs. Morton put her first name up there."

"Oh. I guess so," I agreed. Mrs. Morton is like that. She even told us once that she was forty-one years old. Another time, she mentioned that she wished she had children of her own, but that she didn't get married until she was thirty-five. (At lunch that day, Murray Hamm commented that he wasn't surprised, considering her teeth.) I told her Mother had me when she was thirty-six, but Mrs. Morton just smiled in a sad kind of way. It's not every teacher who will share her real life with a class like that. Most of them try to pretend they're perfect. Or else they think we're too young and stupid to understand.

At the moment, though, I was too worried about the assignment to appreciate Mrs. Morton's first name.

Reggie's gossip column was already a page and a half longer than the maximum and she still had the final weekend roundup to cover. Mrs. Morton made her edit out five different items about Rod Whitman. Some of them dealt with really important stuff, such as "What basketball captain looked super-sharp in his new gray crewneck sweater last Wednesday?" and "Which senior was seen lounging against his locker between classes last week?" My favorite item was written after Rod brushed past Reggie in the lunchroom one day: "Someone special has a new after-shave lotion. It smells like fresh limes on a tropical beach." Mrs. Morton didn't think that was a truly newsworthy fact.

Almost everybody else was ahead of schedule, too. Paul DuBerry had a good rundown of the basketball team, which had a 3–0 record at that time. Some kids were turning in reports and editorials on the President, the neutron bomb, world hunger, all kinds of great things. Even Marjory Warren's article was interesting: "A Day in the Life of a State Senator." Everyone was fascinated when she read it because nobody had the slightest idea what a state senator actually did. It turns out they have quite a bit of power over schools, for one thing.

And then there was me.

"Mrs. Morton," I pleaded one afternoon, "I really don't know what to write about. I was considering a fashion article . . ."

"We already have a fashion article, Summer," Mrs. Morton said, studying my face thoughtfully. I blushed and squirmed as usual. "It's odd," she went on, "I've known you quite a while, but I really don't know much about you. What you like, for instance, or what you don't like."

"I keep a very low profile," I said, quoting something I'd heard once on TV.

Mrs. Morton laughed. "You certainly do," she agreed. "But I think it would be good for you to try an editorial. To take a stand on something important to you."

"I don't like to do that," I murmured, my voice stuck way back in my throat.

"Why not?"

"I don't know. I just don't like to."

Mrs. Morton regarded me a while longer. The fluorescent lights were dancing in her glasses. I concentrated on them so I wouldn't have to think about her looking at me like that.

"The assignment stands," she said, at last. "And it's due in one week, so you'd better get to work on it."

I nodded glumly and left the room. Where was I going to find a topic? I didn't know enough about national politics to write five good sentences. I didn't know beans about local politics. Come to think of it, I didn't know very much about anything. Everybody else did. Dad had his literature. Mother had sports. Douglas had European history. Terry had journalism. Even Reggie had Love. What was wrong with me?

Well, whatever it was, it was going to have to change, I announced to myself. I was getting too old for this sort of nonsense. I threw back my head, clenched my teeth and marched out into the world in search of a topic. A few days later, when I still had absolutely nothing and was on the verge of screaming, hair-tearing panic, my topic found me.

# 4

That fateful afternoon, instead of walking home with Reggie, I had to go all the way across campus to Dad's office. We were going to do some Christmas shopping and then eat out together. Mother was out of town at a physical-education conference.

It was an extremely gray day. The sky looked as if it couldn't hold the snow back another minute. Maybe it would be a white Christmas. Or maybe it would snow too soon and be a slushy, dirty Christmas, which is worse than a Christmas with no snow at all. The trees along the path to Dad's office were all bare, with gnarled branches that looked spooky against the gray sky.

I pulled my parka hood tighter and sped up. Before I knew it, I'd come up behind a couple of women. I could have passed them, but I caught a snatch of their conversation and it held me right where I was—close enough to eavesdrop without being too obvious about it. Not that I'm an eavesdropper ordinarily. In fact, I try very hard to stay out of other people's business. But this particular conversation was about University School, which, in a way, *was* my business.

"And they call themselves a University School. It's disgraceful," the lady in the long brown coat snorted. "But what are you going to do? It's Christmas, it's a tradition, and they don't realize what they're doing."

"Well, maybe that excuses some of them," the other lady said. She was very heavy and was wearing a tan quilted parka. The way the hood came to a point made her look like an enormous football. "But what about the administration? It *is* a state institution, isn't it? Haven't they heard about separation of church and state? The way you describe that program, it sounds illegal. That's exactly what it is, illegal."

"*I* know it and *you* know it, but apparently they don't."

"Or they do and choose to ignore it."

They were quiet for a moment. The lady in the brown coat switched her purse from one shoulder to the other. "It wouldn't be so bad," she said, "if they just sang winter songs. 'Frosty the Snowman,' things like that. But they have it set up with candles and Christmas carols and readings of the Nativity story from the New Testament. It's a religious service, that's what it is. All they need is a minister and they're ready to go. It has absolutely no place in a school."

The other lady nodded. "What are you going to do?" she asked.

"I don't know. Probably nothing. I feel like such a hypocrite when I tell Andrea it's okay to be in that program. I tell her it's like a play. Jews can pretend they're Christians in a play. Christians can pretend they're Jews."

"That I'd like to see. When do they have the program when Christians pretend they're Jews? Or Buddhists or Hindus or even atheists?"

"Wouldn't that be something? And it would be very appropriate, too. After all, this is a university. There are all kinds of people here. They ought to make it a Universal Winter Holiday program."

"Almost every religion and nationality has a winter holiday."

"That's true. Then everybody could participate with a clear conscience. Oh, Milly, do you know what my Andrea said to me the other day? 'Mama,' she said, 'what if they had to practice Jewish songs every day for a month? I bet they wouldn't like it one bit.'"

"Isn't that something? Well, she's in third grade now. She's beginning to realize she's different from the majority."

Andrea's mother shifted her purse again. She must have been carrying rocks in it. "I don't think she'd mind being different," she said. "But that program makes her wonder if maybe *our* kind of different is not as good as *theirs*."

"That's a shame. Have you complained to the principal?"

"And make a martyr of Andrea? It's bad enough she's the only Jew in her class. She doesn't have to be the troublemaker, too."

"I suppose not."

"And besides, I don't think they'd understand. Last December I went to Andrea's class, at the teacher's invitation, and explained to the children about Hanukkah. I went through the whole bit: that Jewish people don't celebrate Christmas, that we have a different winter holiday, that we exchange gifts and light candles and so on and so forth. And after I was finished, the teacher came up to me—this is Mrs. Whiteford, an excellent teacher; Andrea loved her—she came up to thank me for a very interesting program and so on and so forth. And then she asked me if we'd put up our Christmas tree yet!"

"Isn't that incredible?"

"They just don't understand."

"It's not that they're being cruel on purpose, I don't think. They really don't realize."

"Well, that's one big advantage of being part of a minority. You never make the mistake of thinking everybody else is exactly like you."

We were approaching a fork in the road.

"Oh, the library's this way," Andrea's mother told Milly. They started left where I had to go right. "I don't want you to miss the library."

"It's a beautiful campus," Milly remarked.

"Yes, it is. I wish you could have come in the spring. It's absolutely breathtaking. But a winter visit is better than none at all."

Their voices faded away as I continued on to Dad's office. I sat down on a bench in the hall. The building was steaming compared to the cold outside. My glasses fogged up. I didn't bother to wipe them. I didn't even unzip my parka.

What the ladies had said upset me. I never thought about the Jewish kids when we were rehearsing the Christmas program. There aren't any Jewish kids in my class, let alone Hindus or Buddhists. I'm not sure about atheists. But I could see that it must be very unpleasant for all those people. They had to feel terribly left out. And they were right, they *were* left out. Well, if *I* could see that, why couldn't everybody else? Andrea's mother hadn't even tried to explain to anyone. But I could!

There was my editorial! It would be newsworthy, but not too controversial. I mean, who could argue with it? Even the Christian kids were bored with the program, except for the lucky seniors, who didn't have to be in it.

I started getting really excited about the idea. I had a topic at last, and an editorial that might actually do some good. Maybe it would change people's ideas, as Mrs. Morton said editorials sometimes did. She said they were especially effective if people were kind of leaning in that direction to begin with—and we certainly were when it came to changing the Christmas program. And, if what Andrea's mother said was true, that people weren't being mean on purpose, that they just didn't realize what they

35

were doing wrong, then my editorial would be just the thing to bring it to their attention.

By the time Dad came out of his office, I was all fired up. I didn't even notice that I'd been sweating under my parka. Until we went outside, that is, and the layer of sweat next to my skin started to freeze. My teeth chattered.

"You're not getting sick, are you?" Dad asked, turning on the car heater. Cold air blew around my legs.

"I don't think so," I said.

"Good. With Mother gone all weekend, this is no time for either of us to get sick."

The heat was just beginning to thaw me out when we pulled up at the mall. One last run through the cold and I was safely inside. This time I took off my parka. Dad handed me the twenty dollars I'd saved up. We headed off in opposite directions so we could buy surprise gifts. I found a beautiful sky-blue shirt for Douglas and a necklace for Mother. That left $2.96 to spend on poor Dad. His gift would have to wait until I could earn more, either babysitting or—if the weather cooperated—shoveling snow. I browsed in the record store for a while, then met Dad at the hot-dog stand for dinner. Over my pizza hot dog, I tried out my topic on him.

"Did you ever think how the Jews and Buddhists and Hindus feel about our Christmas program at school?" I asked.

"Well, no," he said. "How do they feel?"

"Left out," I mumbled, wiping pizza sauce off my chin with a napkin.

Dad nodded. "Yes, I suppose they would. Interesting point."

I smiled, very pleased with his reaction. Interesting, but not controversial. "I'm going to write an editorial about it for *The Eighth Grade Reporter*," I announced.

Dad looked surprised. "Are you?" he said, a smile twinkling in his eyes, which is what his smiles do rather than spread around the rest of his face. "Following in the old footsteps, huh? That's nice."

His twinkle was nice, too. I liked thinking he was pleased with me. I felt very warm and cozy.

At home, I bounded upstairs to call Reggie from my parents' room. "Reggie," I said, "have you ever thought about how the Jewish people and the Buddhists and all the other minority groups feel about our Christmas program at school?"

"I didn't know we had any Buddhists," she said.

"The Chongs could be. You know, the twins in fifth grade."

"Hmmmm. Could be."

"Well, have you ever thought about it? How they feel about singing Christmas carols for more than a month every year?"

"No. But I know how I feel about it. Bored. I can't stand singing alto. You don't even get the pretty melodies. At least last year I got to sing soprano."

The perfect topic. A newsworthy item, and everybody was safely on my side.

Or so I thought. Brother, was I naive.

# 5

## Reflections on the Christmas Program
### *by Summer Smith*

The Christmas spirit is everywhere. Or is it? True, the city is alive with bright lights and bustling shoppers. Excited children are standing patiently in long lines to tell their secret wishes to Santa Claus.

And at University School, everyone is looking forward to the annual Christmas program. Or are they? Except for curiosity about what surprise the seniors will spring on us, most students approach the daily rehearsals of the Christmas program with moans and groans.

The program has not changed in any way since it first

began. Some people, such as the eighth graders, have been singing the exact same carols in the exact same order for nine straight years. While we love the carols dearly, we often wish for a little variety. Progressing from soprano to alto parts is not really enough.

We understand that the Christmas program is a University School tradition. We do not want to spoil the memories of those who have graduated. But we wish that each year's program could have something special for those who have not yet graduated, other than the seniors. This is especially important because many of us stay here for thirteen years. At some schools, children graduate after sixth grade and again after eighth grade.

This newspaper is the eighth graders' attempt to add their special touch to the events of the season. It has helped us, but there are other things that could be improved, too. For instance, we should all consider the viewpoint of those University School students who are not Christian. Perhaps we could add some Hanukkah songs for our Jewish friends and some Buddhist and Hindu selections as well. In fact, we should make the program more of a winter celebration instead of a religious service because our friends who are not Christian must feel very much left out.

It's too late to change the program this year, but let's all think about it for next year. Until then, a Merry Christmas, a Happy Hanukkah and best wishes for whatever other holiday you may be celebrating. Happy New Year, too.

Mrs. Morton read my article over twice, then settled back in her chair and gazed up at me. A smile twitched around her lips.

"You've made several very valid points here, Summer," she said. She sounded surprised. "I'm pleased. Very pleased."

"Thank you," I said, and breathed a huge sigh of relief as I sank into my seat. Well, that was over.

"Summer?" Mrs. Morton smiled.

"Yes?"

"Perhaps you might say '. . . *some* students approach the daily rehearsals of the Christmas program with moans and groans,' instead of '*most* students.' We really don't know how *most* students feel, do we?"

"No, I guess not. I'll change it."

"Let me," Terry called out. "I'm the editor and that's editing."

Mrs. Morton laughed and passed my article to Terry.

December 19: Right on schedule, the paper went out to the other classes. We all gave Terry three big cheers and he blushed, but you could see he felt terrific about it.

The morning of December 20: The Chong twins beat up one of their classmates for calling them Buddhists. It turns out they are Catholic.

The afternoon of December 20: Andrea's mother had to come and take her home early. A gang of other third graders had surrounded her in the cafeteria, insisting she hated Christmas because she was Jewish.

December 21: First thing in the morning, our principal, Dr. Kyle, spoke over the intercom: "Mrs. Morton, please come to my office immediately."

Mrs. Morton looked surprised, then asked Reggie to finish taking roll. "If I'm not back when the bell rings," she told us, "just go on to your first-period class. I'll see you later for English."

40

"What do you suppose he wants?" everybody started asking everybody else the minute Mrs. Morton was out the door.

"Maybe he wants to compliment her on the newspaper," Terry offered hopefully. He had every right to be proud. It was a very good newspaper.

In a few minutes, the bell rang and we all shuffled out. About halfway up the hall, Mrs. Morton tore past us. Her cheeks were flaming red, and she looked absolutely wild-eyed.

Reggie and I and a few others stared after her in amazement. She whipped into her classroom and slammed the door shut behind her.

"What in the world . . . ?" Terry said.

We all looked at each other and shrugged. Reggie wondered if we should go back and check on Mrs. Morton. But the next bell rang, so we hurried on to math.

English came right after lunch. Reggie, Terry, and I gobbled our lasagna (that's what the menu said it was, anyway) and raced up to Mrs. Morton's room. She wasn't there. She didn't come in until all the other kids had arrived. There was dead silence the minute she walked in. She looked very pale now and her eyelids kept fluttering. She poked her glasses up on her nose and looked out over our heads when she spoke. Her voice sounded odd, kind of quivery.

"Eighth graders, I'm afraid I have some bad news. Apparently, Summer's very fine editorial has upset several people connected with University School. Dr. Kyle has asked me—no, *demanded*, that I tell Summer to

41

write an apology for her statements and distribute it to the parents who will attend the Christmas program this Friday."

My mouth fell open. I couldn't believe what I was hearing.

"But, Mrs. Morton," Terry began. Without looking his way, Mrs. Morton raised a hand to stop him and continued talking.

"Of course, I told him that was out of the question. Summer has nothing for which to apologize. Her article contained no erroneous facts and, as for her opinions, she is entitled to them. In fact, they are protected by the First Amendment of the Constitution of the United States of America. However, Dr. Kyle felt he had to insist on the apology and rather than be a party to such unconstitutional and unfair censorship, I have chosen to resign my position at University School."

With that, Mrs. Morton slumped down into her chair, as if she'd been shot.

I was too shocked to react. I was sure I hadn't heard right. Or was this a nightmare and I'd wake up any minute? My editorial? My safe, interesting but not *too* interesting editorial? Me, Summer Smith, write an apology and distribute it at the Christmas program? Suddenly, my stomach was churning. I thought I was going to be sick. All around me, like a hurricane wind, voices roared.

"It's not true!"

"That's crazy."

"You can't resign, Mrs. Morton."

42

"What are we going to do?"

I sat staring at Mrs. Morton without saying a word. Suddenly, I felt the skin on the back of my neck creep, as if someone were staring at me. The roar of voices was fading, and as I turned my head, it stopped completely. Row after row of eyes drilled into my face. It was *my* fault. They all thought Mrs. Morton was resigning because of *me*.

I started to babble. "I didn't mean it. I didn't. I'm sorry, really I am."

Then there was a loud crash. We all jumped and gasped and spun around to face Mrs. Morton. She was picking up her huge dictionary off the floor. She looked furious. She slammed the dictionary down again, but on the desk this time.

"Just one minute," she bellowed, glaring from one face to the next. "Just one minute here. I will not have you accusing Summer. I will not have you persecuting her. Do you think I quit my job so you could do that? I've done what I had to do because I believe in Summer and in her right to print that editorial. I refuse to allow you to turn on her like a pack of hyenas. Don't you realize what's at stake here? Freedom of the press, that's what. You put together a newspaper and you did a fine job of it, and I expect you to defend that newspaper against unjust criticism. Is that clear?"

Heads hung low. A few people mumbled.

"I said, is that clear?" Mrs. Morton repeated.

"Yes, Mrs. Morton," we chanted.

I slid my eyes sideways toward Reggie. She winked at

43

me. That made me feel a little better, but not much. Slowly, I raised my hand.

"Yes, Summer?"

"I'm sorry to have caused you so much trouble," I said. My voice sounded even more quivery than Mrs. Morton's had.

"There is no need to apologize, Summer. I'm proud of what you did. I want you to be proud, too."

"Well, but if I'm not going to write an apology and distribute it at the Christmas program, what *am* I going to do?"

"Nothing."

"You mean not be in the program?" It sounded like a great idea to me. I'd just stay home that day. Or maybe for the rest of my life.

"No, you'll go right ahead and perform in the program as planned. With your head held high and your classmates there to support you."

"Sure, Summer, we'll be there," Terry said. A few others agreed. But not everybody.

I swallowed hard. "I'm not good at this kind of thing, Mrs. Morton," I said. My voice sounded so small, like a two-year-old's. That's about how the rest of me felt, too.

"I know, Summer. It won't be easy. But sometimes we have to stand up for what's right, no matter how hard it is for us."

"Us?" I squeaked. "Will you be there?"

"Friday will be my last day. Let's make it a proud one, okay?"

"Okay," I whispered, as her face swam away from me on a wave of tears.

"Summer," Mrs. Morton said, very softly. I looked in her direction, but I really couldn't see her. "I hate to say this to you now, but Dr. Kyle would like to see you in his office."

"Oh, no," I whimpered.

"Can I go with her, Mrs. Morton?" Reggie offered.

"Me, too," Terry added. "I'm her editor in chief." What brave, true friends.

"No, I'm afraid not. Summer, he's just going to tell you the same thing he told me. To write an apology. You know how I feel about it. But to be perfectly fair, I have to let you make your own decision. I shouldn't dictate to you about how you should act. If you'd rather go ahead with the apology, then do so. I will understand. Really I will. Now, you'd better get over there."

Somehow I stood up and walked out of the room.

# 6

I don't remember the trip, but I did end up sitting on the wooden bench in the waiting room outside Dr. Kyle's office. There must have been a hundred times when I'd delivered messages to that office for my teachers and seen kids in trouble sitting on that bench. I'd always thought they looked like convicts in the electric chair, waiting for Dr. Kyle to pull the switch. I'd always been thankful it wasn't me sitting there. But now, it was.

The bench was every bit as hard and uncomfortable as it looked. I bet Dr. Kyle planned it that way. Mrs. O'Malley, Dr. Kyle's secretary, nodded at me, then went back to her typing. A couple of little kids came in, one clutching a note in her hand. They both stared at me, goggle-eyed, all the way to Mrs. O'Malley's desk and all the way back to the door again. They disappeared out the door. Then one little eye returned for a last peek at the condemned criminal. I stuck out my tongue and the little eye vanished.

The buzzer sounded on Mrs. O'Malley's desk.

"You may go in now," she told me.

I concentrated on putting one foot in front of the other and managed to cross the room. I rapped on Dr. Kyle's door.

"Come in."

I opened the door and a stale tobacco smell seeped out. My nose twitched. So, he smoked on the sly, did he? Or had he recently had a visitor who smoked?

"Sit down, Summer," Dr. Kyle said, indicating a chair across the desk from his. I noted that the ashtray, empty but smudged, was at his edge of the desk. He was the culprit, all right.

Dr. Kyle was in his shirt sleeves, which surprised me. In fact, I felt embarrassed, as if I'd caught him in his underwear. I'd never seen him without a jacket on before. He never walked around the halls in his shirt sleeves, and the only other time I'd been in his office was when I first came to University School as a kindergartner. I remember thinking the office was a huge, dark cave and that Dr. Kyle, with his big ears and fringe of gray hair around a bald dome, was an enormous ogre. Now I saw that the office was really rather small and cramped, what with the desk and a sofa and chairs and the bookshelves covering two walls. The other two walls were dark wood paneling and did make things gloomy. Dr. Kyle, of course, grew smaller every year and turned out to be more of a not-too-friendly elf than an ogre.

"I suppose Mrs. Morton has informed you of the situation," he said.

"Yes," said a tiny voice temporarily occupying my mouth.

"Are you fully aware of the problems your editorial has caused?"

"Well, I know the Chong twins had a fight and Andrea in the third grade got teased and had to go home."

"And that's all?"

"Yes."

"Unfortunately, Mrs. Morton did not stay long enough to hear the full story." He sighed deeply and picked up a pen. Rat-a-tat, rat-a-tat it went, like the drumroll before an execution. Finally, he stopped tapping and spoke again. "Dr. Ivan Transkill. Do you know that name?" He stared me straight in the eye for what seemed like a very long time. It nearly killed me, but I managed to stare right back. I knew I'd look shifty and dishonest if I flinched.

"No," I replied, hoping that not recognizing the name proved that I wasn't guilty. Guilty of what?

Dr. Kyle looked away, breaking the deadlock, thank goodness. "For your information," he said, "Dr. Transkill is on the Board of Trustees of this University. Do you know what that means?"

"Not exactly. Um, the Board of Trustees is kind of in charge of everything, isn't it?"

"Something very much like that. Well, Dr. Transkill also graduated from University School. Dr. Transkill's father and mother graduated from University School. Dr. Transkill's grandfather was one of its very first instructors. So, the present Dr. Transkill is an important, influential man, indeed."

"I see."

"I don't think you do. Not yet. There are two interesting bits of information about Dr. Transkill's grandfather that you need to know. First, he was very wealthy. He donated almost all of the money required to found University School. It would have been named after him, but he was a modest man and didn't really care for the sound of Transkill School."

An insane giggle forced its way up my throat. Panicked, I pretended to have a coughing fit until I could force it back down again. Dr. Kyle eyed me with disapproval. He waited until I finished coughing, then continued.

"The second fact about Dr. Transkill's grandfather is that he was our first music teacher, and that he organized the first University School Christmas program, over fifty years ago. And the University School Christmas program has never been changed since that very first program. It is our tribute to the founder of this school. And you, Miss Smith, approach it with moans and groans. Do you realize that an insult to the Christmas program is an insult to the entire Transkill family, living and dead?"

"I didn't mean to . . ."

49

Dr. Kyle leaned toward me for emphasis. "Do you *realize* that the present Dr. Transkill has no children and that the entire Transkill fortune—which is considerable—has been willed to the University upon Dr. Transkill's death? Unless, of course, Dr. Transkill decides to change his will for some small reason."

"Well, I . . ."

"Do you realize that it's more than the Chong twins and Andrea Caplan?"

"Well, yes . . ."

"And will you print an apology and distribute it at the traditional Christmas program this Friday?"

My mouth was awfully dry. I licked my lips and tried to work up a little saliva. "Could I think it over?" I rasped.

"What?"

I cleared my throat and tried again. "Could I please think it over?"

Dr. Kyle stood up to his full height, which isn't that much taller than some kids in my class. He took another deep breath and tucked his shirt in over his midriff bulge, as Mother calls it. I looked away, embarrassed. I'm not accustomed to seeing principals get dressed in front of me.

His shirt arranged, Dr. Kyle walked over to one of the bookshelves and slowly ran a finger along a blue binding. Then he turned back to me. An angry red splotch had spread across his face, except for his lips, which formed a thin white line.

"I will be calling your parents about this," he announced.

I winced. "Well, I'd like to talk to them, too, while I'm thinking things over."

Dr. Kyle's bushy gray brows shot upward. Oh, wow, I thought, did I sound fresh? I didn't mean to. I seemed to be doing a lot of things I didn't mean to, lately. But he just looked away and said, "Very well. You may go."

"Thank you."

I slid off the chair and got out of there fast.

# 7

Reggie and Terry marched me home from school, one on each side, like bodyguards. Other than commenting on the snow, which was thick and wet and already sticking to the pavement, we were quiet and grim. They didn't hang around long when we got to my house. Dad's car was very obviously in the driveway.

"Good luck, Summer," Reggie said, with a quick hug. I almost laughed when I looked at her face. She couldn't have worn a sadder expression if she'd led me to the guillotine.

"Thanks, Reg," I said, trying to sound braver than I felt.

Terry shook my hand solemnly. I knew what he was thinking: Woodward and Bernstein and Watergate.

"Someday you can write a best seller about this," I told him. For a second, his face lit up, as if he believed me. Then, realizing he shouldn't get too happy about my fate, he just nodded and wished me luck.

Somehow I felt as if I were comforting the two of them instead of the other way around. Well, maybe I could afford to. After I'd survived the visit to Dr. Kyle's office, my jitters settled down a lot. I don't mean to say I enjoyed the experience. It's not among the Ten Greatest Moments of my life. But it wasn't that bad. I still had all my fingers and toes and I was still breathing. In fact, I was pretty much the same old Summer Smith, except for an occasional flip-flop in my stomach whenever I really thought about what I'd gotten myself into.

The evening paper was soggy under its light coating of snow. I scooped it up, said a last good-bye and ran up the stairs to the porch.

"Call me later," Reggie yelled from halfway up the block.

"Okay," I yelled back. I checked the mailbox. It was empty. I knew Dad would have already taken in the mail, but I'm so crazy about mail I always hope for a second delivery. Or maybe a letter that got delivered to a neighbor's house by mistake and then was brought over and slipped into our box. I have to hope for second deliveries because I never get anything in the first delivery. Except at my birthday, of course, but that doesn't count.

Dad was sitting at his rolltop desk at the side of the living room. I love that desk. It's huge and very old and has a bunch of tiny drawers and compartments. Once, when I was younger, I read about somebody finding a fortune behind a secret door in an old rolltop. I spent days tapping and pushing every inch of Dad's desk. No luck. I still give it a little tap now and then.

Dad was sorting his mail. That's how much he gets, enough to have to sort it out into several piles. When I was little, he used to give me all his junk mail. I thought it was terrifically important and carried it around with me all day. Now I don't even get that.

Dad peered at me over his glasses when I walked in, eyes a-twinkle. He must have been chewing pretty hard on his pipe stem because the pipe was jiggling in his mouth. Was he laughing?

"Hi," I offered, hopefully. It came out sounding like a question.

"Hail the conquering journalist!" he said. He was laughing, all right. Dad doesn't exactly roar with laughter. He twinkles his eyes and jiggles his pipe. A smile, on the other hand, equals the twinkle minus the jiggle.

"Dr. Kyle called you?"

"Dr. Kyle did."

"And you're not angry with me?"

"Why should I be? The article was accurate, grammatically correct, and properly spelled."

I grinned and hung up my parka.

"So why would I be angry with *you?*" he went on, landing hard on the word "you."

"You're not angry at Mrs. Morton, are you?" I asked. "It's not her fault."

"Absolutely not. If I'm angry at anyone, it's Dr. Kyle."

Dad's eyebrows wiggled together over his nose. Tornado warning. Head for the cellar. It made me feel queasy inside, even though I wasn't the one he was angry with. With whom he was angry. I just can't stand it when anybody's angry at anybody, especially Dad. He may not roar with laughter, but he can get up a pretty good growl with anger. In fact, he can rattle the chandelier in the dining room. And my bones.

"Imagine that man asking you to print an apology! And why? Because some ancient Transkill *might* be offended by your honest opinion. Such cowardice!"

"You mean Dr. Transkill hasn't even read my editorial?"

"Well, actually he has read it. But Dr. Kyle asked for your apology *before* Transkill read it. He's called me twice, Dr. Kyle has. Once at the office and once again just before you came in. Dr. Transkill read the article this afternoon and felt that he really didn't have the time or the desire to trouble himself about an eighth-grade newspaper distributed within the school."

"Then there's no problem," I cried, starting toward Dad's neck for a hug of relief.

Dad held up a hand to ward me off. "Is that the evening paper you brought in?" he asked.

"Yes. What about it?"

"I've been told there's a pertinent article at the bottom of page one, column five."

Completely puzzled, I pulled the rubber band off the paper and located the bottom of page one:

## U. SCHOOL TEACHER RESIGNS OVER
## NEWSPAPER FRACAS

English instructor Virginia Morton resigned her position at University School early today. The resignation came in response to a demand that one of her students apologize for editorial statements printed in *The Eighth Grade Reporter*, a class newspaper. The editorial questioned the appropriateness of the traditional University School Christmas program.

Mrs. Morton, a tenured faculty member for six years, refused to reveal whether her resignation was forced or voluntary. She did indicate, however, that she planned to consult a lawyer about the situation.

The student involved, Summer Smith, is the daughter of Olympic champion Angela Gregory Smith and literary critic Douglas Marshall Smith. Both parents teach at Middletown University. Neither Miss Smith nor her parents could be reached for comment.

The rest of the article described the Christmas program, quoted my editorial, and kind of suggested the whole city turn out on Friday to judge for themselves. It ended with a reminder that Mother had won five gold medals and made Olympic history over twenty years ago.

I sank into a chair and wished I could go right on sinking until I melted into the core of the earth.

"Dad, would you mind very much if I dropped out of University School? I could go to public school . . ."

"Out of the question. I don't . . ."

56

All of a sudden, the back door swung open and slammed shut.

"Where is she?" Mother's voice shrieked. "Summer, are you here?"

"We're in the living room," Dad called.

Mother appeared in the archway between the dining and living rooms. She whipped her knit cap off her head. Her long hair went flying from the electricity.

"Summer Smith, what have you done now?" she demanded.

"What do you mean, *now?*" Dad asked. "What had she done before?"

Mother glared at him. "Please do not quibble with me about my choice of words," she snapped. "Do you realize that I have had a hysterical woman in my office for the last hour, ranting and raving and practically chewing the paint off the walls?"

"Who?" I wondered.

"Mrs. Jack Caplan, that's who."

"Who's that?" Dad wanted to know.

"I'm sure Summer knows who that is," Mother said. She was tearing at the buttons on her coat. "Oh, damn," she wailed and stuck her little finger into her mouth. "Now I've broken my nail."

I sighed. "I guess Mrs. Jack Caplan is Andrea Caplan's mother."

"Bingo," Mother said, on her way to the bedroom for a nail file.

"Why was she ranting and raving and chewing paint?" Dad called.

Mother came back, scraping at her broken nail savagely.

"Because her little girl refuses to go back to school. Apparently children read Summer's article and began persecuting her. Telling her she hated Christmas because she was Jewish."

"Well, that's very foolish," Dad said. "But it might be better in the long run. Sometimes it's good to get ideas like that out in the open where people can examine them and learn something."

"Well, Mrs. Caplan does not agree," Mother said. She blew the filings off her finger and examined the nail from all angles. "Mrs. Caplan thinks the less said the better. She does not want her daughter to be a martyr, she said. She herself grew up during World War Two and had swastikas and 'Dirty Jew' painted all over her house by neighborhood bullies." Mother's voice was rising and she was waving the file around like a fencing foil. "Mrs. Caplan says she has suffered quite enough, thank you, and would prefer to be left alone. She certainly wants her daughter left alone."

"I was only trying to help," I said, weakly.

"The Caplans do not want your help," Mother insisted. "They want to be left alone. And I can't say that I blame them. At this point, I'd like to be left alone, too!"

Hot tears suddenly bubbled over my eyelids. "Then why did she say what she said when I heard her and got the idea for the article?" I wailed. "I heard her with my own ears. She said that the Christmas program was illegal. She said it had absolutely no place in a school."

"When did you hear her say that?" Dad asked.

I sniffled back my tears and wiped my cheeks with my hands.

"While I was walking behind her one afternoon, on the way to your office. She was talking to a friend and they were both going on and on about the program. And how Christians didn't understand how they hurt other people's feelings. Well, I understood, once I heard her talk about it. So I thought if I made other people aware of it, they'd understand, too. You can't understand if nobody even tells you something's wrong."

Dad nodded. I didn't look at Mother. I could hear her scritch-scritching away at her nail, though. It made my skin crawl.

"What I *can't* understand," I went on, "is why people like Mrs. Caplan don't do anything about it if they're unhappy about something."

The phone rang. "Oh, you'll find out why," Mother said over her shoulder as she headed for the kitchen. "You'll find out."

Dad and I were quiet while she picked up the receiver and said hello. Suddenly she slammed down the receiver so hard the little bell inside the phone chimed.

Dad stood up and started toward her. "What's wrong?" he asked.

"Some foul-mouthed idiot just called me a Jew-loving waste!"

"A waste?" I echoed. "What does that mean?"

Dad sank back into his chair. "He must have said 'waspe.' I think he meant 'WASP.' White-Anglo-Saxon-

Protestant." Dad's pipe danced a jig. A kind of strangled chuckle came out of his throat.

"Oh, laugh, laugh," Mother said, throwing her arms in the air. "They'll be calling all day and night now. They'll be burning crosses on our lawn." She spun around to face me. "And *that*, my darling daughter, is why people don't do anything about things they know are wrong. It's too damn much trouble. And it's *dangerous*."

"Oh, come on," Dad said. "We've had exactly one caller and he couldn't even get his epithet straight."

"Oh, terrific. Oh, wonderful," Mother yelped. "I should have gotten that creep's name and address. Then you could have corrected his spelling and sent him a grade."

Dad twinkled up at her. She whipped her face away from him, but she was biting her lip. Then she was snickering. Suddenly she flopped on the sofa, laughing like a loon. I started to laugh, too. Finally, Mother sat up and wiped tears from her eyes. "Jew-loving waste," she said, shaking her head. "I swear, some people . . ."

Dad tapped out his old tobacco and refilled his pipe.

"Well, if you feel better now, I think we'd better decide what we're going to do about this situation."

"All right," Mother agreed. "I'm sorry I came home loaded for bear. But that Caplan woman really upset me. And there were reporters calling, too. My secretary didn't put them through, thank goodness, because of Mrs. Caplan."

Dad nodded. "Mrs. Caplan won't be the last. But we'll be ready, now. I hope you'll join me, Angela, in supporting Summer. This isn't going to be easy for any of us, but she'll get the worst of it. What she did was right, though, and I intend to stand by her to the bitter end."

Mother ran both hands through her hair and sighed. "Yes, I suppose that's all we can do."

"Thank you," I said, because I knew I was supposed to. But I didn't feel that overjoyed about their support, especially not to the bitter end. I was really kind of hoping they'd take me to Timbuktu for a forty-year vacation.

# 8

When I woke up the next morning, I swallowed hard five or six times. I was hoping for that scratchy feeling you get before a sore throat. They say if you're very upset emotionally, you can get sick physically. By my calculations, I should have had cancer. I didn't even have tonsilitis. I crawled out of bed and put on my glasses, then checked the window. Plenty of snow, but not enough to cancel school. No escape.

A doomed woman, I dragged myself through the morning routine, in and out of drawers, closet, bathroom, and then downstairs.

"Good morning," Dad said, slipping seven-grain bread into the toaster for me.

Mother put hot chocolate at my place as I sat down. What a nice warm sweetness it was, all soft brown with happy little bubbles on top. I wanted to dive in and pull the happy little bubbles over me.

"You okay?" Mother asked.

I shrugged. "I didn't sleep much. I have to tell Dr. Kyle my decision today. About the apology."

"You have made your decision, haven't you?" Dad asked.

"I don't know," I admitted, stirring the hot chocolate slowly. The spoon made a depression in the center, like a whirlpool. A perfect little spot for me. I'd disappear down the hole like a rabbit. "I don't like to have everyone angry at me, Dad. I really don't. And Dr. Kyle is going to be *wild* now that the story is in the city paper. Probably Dr. Transkill is chewing paint off *his* walls, like Mother said yesterday."

"*As* Mother said yesterday. No one enjoys making people angry, Summer. The point is, how far are you willing to compromise your beliefs in order to avoid anger?"

Pretty far, I thought. But I knew better than to say it.

"On the other hand, I don't want to disappoint Mrs. Morton," I added. I'd spent a good deal of the night mentally galloping in many directions and arriving at the same conclusion: whatever I decided to do, somebody wasn't going to like it. "Mrs. Morton thinks we ought to stand up for our newspaper. And, of course, you do, too."

"Wait a minute," Mother said. She handed me a tub of margarine and flipped my toast onto a plate. Then she served three bowls of an unbelievably strange-looking grayish-brown mush. I didn't bother to ask what it was. I knew what it was. The health-food store's latest creation. Liquid energy or semisolid vitamins or maybe fresh-ground kelp. I sighed and dug in, but I noticed that Dad was simply ignoring it.

"I said I'd support you," Mother went on, "whatever you decided. But I want you to know my full opinion. You don't have to agree, but at least consider it. I think it's ridiculous to have this enormous to-do over a child's editorial in a children's newspaper. It's just not that big a deal. Your decision will not change the course of history. Life will go on with your apology or without it. So, if I were you, I'd write that apology and save a lot of people a lot of trouble. The three of us, especially."

"Angela, I wish . . ."

"Douglas, please let me finish. All you have to do, Summer, is say that in the excitement of contributing an article to your class newspaper you got carried away and made exaggerated statements for which you are sorry."

"But, Angela, that's not true . . ."

"Then she can write something similar that *is* true. I'm not dictating to her. I am merely telling her what I would do, if the decision were mine to make."

"Which it is not," Dad insisted.

"Which it is not," Mother agreed.

We ate—or didn't eat—the rest of the meal in silence. The three bears, I thought. Only it wasn't a cute little girl with golden locks messing up our house. It was a short ogre with a gray fringe. I concentrated very hard on my food so I wouldn't have to think about anything else. Unless you've tried it yourself, you cannot imagine how unpleasant it is to concentrate very hard on chewing mush.

The first thing I noticed when I walked into the classroom was a weird expression on Marjory Warren's face. And on a few other faces, too. Everyone looked away as soon as I came in. The next thing I noticed was a rumpled scrap of notebook paper on my desk. I opened it up and read, "JEW!" The letters were smudgy. I crumpled the paper up and very carefully walked toward the wastepaper basket next to Mrs. Morton's desk. It was not bad to be a Jew, I told myself. Then why did I feel so *squirmy* inside? As if someone had thrown something at me, something hateful and ugly, like a fistful of mud.

Jew. It wasn't the word itself. It was the way they meant it, whoever wrote the note. That was the hateful and ugly part. It hurt. I felt wounded deep inside. I stood at the basket with the paper in my hand, thinking about how much I hurt. It was creeping over me like slow waves coming up from my insides and out to my face and fingertips. An aching, at first. I felt like a lonely little kid, that aching feeling when you're very small and something awful happens and you feel so alone and helpless and sad. All this, I thought, and I'm not even Jewish! What must it feel like when you *are* Jewish? Or black? Or Oriental? The waves got stronger and stronger and then the feeling

65

changed. I was angry. I was furious. I was disgusted and filled with rage. I spun around to find everyone's eyes on me. I sought out Marjory Warren's face and she quickly looked away.

"Did you write this?" I demanded. She kept her face lowered, but other kids were doing the same. I was shaking, but I was too angry to care. "If you did," I went on, "and this goes for everybody who was in on it, then I just want you to know something. I wish I *were* a Jew. I'd be proud of it. And if you hated me for it, I'd be even prouder, because it would just show what idiots you are."

"What's going on?" Mrs. Morton asked from the doorway. I held out the note and she took it and read it. Her face went white.

"Where did you get this?" she asked, her voice barely a whisper.

"It was on my desk when I came in this morning."

"I see. Please sit down," she said, between clenched teeth.

After I sat down, I realized I was trembling like crazy. I wondered if anybody ever had died from acute trembling.

Mrs. Morton paced the floor for a while, not looking at us. Her eyes were blinking rapidly, and she was taking deep breaths as if she was fighting back tears. Everyone sat and watched her without a word. I sneaked a glance at Reggie. She shrugged, wide-eyed.

Finally, Mrs. Morton sat on the corner of her desk. Her eyes wandered from one person to the next as if she were searching for something.

"This note was on *my* desk when I came in this

66

morning," she said, very quietly. "I crumpled it up and threw it in the wastepaper basket. Obviously, someone in this class wrote it, because that someone knew enough to take the crumpled paper out of the basket and put it on Summer's desk. That person—or those persons—are cowardly, I must say, but that is not an unusual trait in a bigot. In fact, I believe it is almost a requirement. At any rate, whoever you are, you should have quit while you were ahead. I am a Jew. Summer is not."

There was a buzzing in the classroom. I suddenly found myself standing up. A gigantic lump formed in my throat. How dare anyone hurt Mrs. Morton like that? How stupid! Idiotic! Cruel! I hated those people, whoever they were. I wanted to kill them.

"What is it, Summer?" Mrs. Morton was asking.

"What?" I said, as if I'd been jolted out of a dream. Why was I standing up?

"Did you want to say something?" Mrs. Morton asked.

"Oh. No. I'm sorry. I . . ." I suddenly realized my fingernails were digging into the palms of my hands. I fell back into my seat. Then my hand, with purple half-moons on its palm, shot into the air. "Yes, I do want to say something. I want to say that I'm not going to write an apology. I believe in what I said and I'm not one bit sorry for it, and I'm willing to . . . to take the consequences."

Terry cheered. Alone. Mrs. Morton gave me a sad smile.

"That is a very courageous stand to take, Summer. But the truth of the matter is, your apology is no longer required. Since the matter has reached the city newspaper, an apology to the school community would be too little too late, you see."

Reggie raised her hand. "Mrs. Morton, are you going to court over this?"

"I don't know. I have to consult further with my lawyer."

"But do you still have to leave after tomorrow?" Terry wanted to know.

"Yes, I'm afraid so."

"Why don't we stage a protest?" Terry announced suddenly. "Why don't we all refuse to be in the Christmas program? There'd be a big hole right in the middle where we're supposed to stand."

"We could march into the gym with our candles and everything," Reggie put in, "but instead of turning toward our places, we could keep marching right out the other door."

"Could we do it, Mrs. Morton?" Terry pleaded.

Mrs. Morton started to speak, but Marjory butted in.

"*I'm* going to be in the program," she said. "I like it."

"If I tried a stunt like that," Murray Hamm muttered, "my parents would kill me."

More and more kids agreed with that. It was obvious that Terry and Reggie were the only ones with guts enough to protest. And I, as usual, was the only one who hadn't given an opinion.

"There is no way I could condone something like that," Mrs. Morton said. "I want to make that very clear. In fact, I don't even want you to mention it again in my presence. I'm in enough hot water as it is."

"We wouldn't get arrested if we did it, would we?" Terry asked.

Mrs. Morton laughed. "No. But you wouldn't have my approval. I have to repeat that. It would be your decision and on your conscience and the consequences, as Summer so aptly put it, would be yours to suffer. Now could we please drop the subject?"

Terry and Reggie looked at each other and then at me. Oh, no, I thought, what now?

The bell rang, but I was not saved by it. Terry and Reggie pestered me all the way down the hall.

"We have to do it," Terry said. "For Mrs. Morton's sake."

"She said she could never condone it," I reminded them.

"That's what she *said*," Reggie put in, "but it's not what she *meant*."

"How do you know what she meant?"

"I just do."

"So do I," Terry agreed. "She told you you were taking a courageous stand by not printing that apology. She'd think the same of us if we walked out of the program."

"Then why didn't she say so?" I demanded.

"Because she couldn't," Terry insisted. "She'd lose her job."

"She's already lost her job!"

"Not if she wins in court."

"She may not even go to court."

"Well, at least she's trying," Reggie insisted. "She's not just letting the matter drop. And neither should we."

"Don't you see," Terry began, as if he were explaining the situation to a two-year-old. "When this issue was just inside the school, Kyle could boss her around. But now that it's public news, it's a whole different ball game. And our protest would keep it public. You can bet there'll be reporters at that program."

"A public scandal," I muttered. I was getting a headache from the two of them bombarding my ears. "Here comes Rod," I added, hoping to change the subject.

Reggie improved her posture slightly, until Rod passed by, but otherwise she stuck to the problem at hand. Could it be she loved Mrs. Morton even more than she loved Rod Whitman?

"Look, Summer," she said, "it was your article that started this mess, and it was your desk they put that note on. You can't back out now."

Suddenly, a nasty thought occurred to me. "Are you doing this just to get Rod's attention?" I demanded.

"No, I am not," Reggie snapped. "That's a rotten thing to say. I'm doing it for Mrs. Morton, and I thought I was doing it for *you*." But something told me the side benefit appealed to her, now that I'd brought it up. Dumb move.

"*I'm* sure not doing it to impress Rod," Terry said. "But I'm doing it whether or not you join me."

"Me, too," Reggie said.

"Could I think about it for a while?" I asked. That approach was coming in pretty handy lately.

"Okay," Terry said, "but don't take forever. We've got to get this thing organized."

70

"Okay," I agreed. I'd never been so happy to get to math class in my entire life.

I thought about it all day, especially when I caught people giving me funny looks in the hall and in class. All kinds of people, big and little, first graders and teachers. I was definitely University School's Topic of the Day. The whole school seemed to be dividing into two camps: For Summer and Against Summer. And it looked as if the Againsts outnumbered the Fors about a hundred to one.

I thought about it all afternoon, while I shoveled snow for two widows on our block. It certainly made the work go fast.

I thought about it lying in bed that night. And all I could figure was that whether or not I joined the protest, I was going to be more deeply in trouble than ever. It had all started with me and it would all end with me, no matter what I did now. The bitter end, as Dad had put it. Oh, we Smiths certainly have a way with words.

# 9

I don't know what Mother served for breakfast on End-of-the-World Friday. I could barely get my eyelids unglued, I'd slept so little.

"How's my journalist on her day of days?" Dad asked, the voice of holiday cheer himself.

"Not great," I mumbled.

"You know, I was thinking, you really hit the jackpot on your first time out. I've been criticizing things for years, and the worst that ever happened was an angry phone call or two. A few unpleasant letters. Nothing nearly as exciting as the Christmas Program Caper."

My poor bloodshot eyeballs struggled to focus on him. Did he know what Reggie and Terry were planning? Impossible. He had to be talking about the editorial hoopla itself. Little did he know that part was soon to become old news.

"There was a critic, once," he mused, "I can't remember the details, but he gave a play a shattering review and the director, I think it was, barged into his private club and shot him."

I dropped my spoon into my whatever-it-was.

"Didn't kill him, I don't think. No, I'm pretty sure he didn't."

Weakly, I retrieved my spoon and went through the motions of consuming health products. Not that I was hungry. I was actually more than a little sick to my stomach. But Mother keeps a very strict vitamin schedule, and not eating leads to a discussion that is simply not worth the trouble. As soon as I safely could, I excused myself and left the table.

"Good luck," Mother wished me. "It's going to be a little rough today."

A *little?* If only she knew.

"All eyes will be upon you," Dad reminded me, as if I needed reminding. "Stand tall."

"I'll try." I bundled up and started out the door.

"Are you sure you don't want us to be there?" Dad called after me. "We could cancel our classes. Hardly anyone shows up the day before Christmas vacation anyway."

"Oh, no. Don't do that. It's okay. Really. 'Bye."

Reggie and Terry were waiting for me on the corner, stamping their feet and huffing great puffs of steam like a pair of angry bulls. Or dragons.

"Well?" Reggie said. "What did you decide?"

"I don't know."

"How can you not know?" Terry wailed. "The program starts at nine thirty." The snow made our voices sound odd, kind of hollow. Dreamlike. Oh, wouldn't that be nice? No such luck.

"I just don't know," I repeated. "Listen, did either of you talk to your parents about this?"

"Are you kidding?" Reggie asked. "Why would I do that?"

"I did," Terry said. "I told my father all about it."

"What did he say?" I wanted to know.

"He said, 'Give 'em hell, Terry.'"

"Did he really?"

"Yup."

"You have a great father," Reggie said.

"I know."

Terry used to have a great mother, too, but she died when we were in third grade. She had a heart attack right at the oven, in the middle of baking cookies. She used to bake cookies all the time—not from a mix either—and Reggie and I would stop in after school for a snack almost every day. When we found out about her heart attack, we thought she'd died of baking cookies. We felt terrible for a long time, until Terry explained it to us better. We were very young.

We were quiet for a while as we trudged toward school. Maybe they were thinking about Terry's mother, too.

New snow had fallen overnight. Everything was so white and quiet, I could hardly stand it.

The school soon loomed ahead of us. You'd think they'd cancel classes with the weather this bad, I thought. A fresh layer of snow can be very treacherous. Doesn't anybody realize that? There could be invisible patches of ice underneath. I wished I were an invisible patch of ice.

"Well, are you or aren't you?" Terry demanded, outside our homeroom door.

"Terry, I just don't know," I whimpered. "I can't make up my mind. I'm scared. And I'm all mixed up. In some ways, I think I might as well go ahead and do it. But in other ways, I really don't want to. I don't want to get into any more trouble."

"Oh, brother," Reggie groaned.

"Well, listen, here's our plan," Terry said, hunching over like a spy delivering nuclear secrets, "just in case you decide to come along. We march in just as we've rehearsed it until we get to the center of the gym. Then, instead of turning toward our seats, we blow out our candles and march straight ahead and out the far door. And we chant, 'We want Mrs. Morton, we want Mrs. Morton.'"

"Oh," I said, suddenly sick to my stomach.

"What do you mean 'oh'?" Reggie demanded. "Don't you get the symbolism?"

"What symbolism?"

"When we blow out the candles. It means Mrs. Morton is a candle that's been blown out of our lives."

"Very clever," I muttered.

"Terry has to go first, because that's where his place is

in line. But I'll fall into step right behind him. I'm just three people back. And then there's you."

They both looked at me, their faces anxious and pleading. I could hardly stand it. I concentrated on their noses, which were still red from the cold and a little moist.

"It won't make a difference in what I do," Reggie said, slowly, earnestly, "but it would help to know you'll be there behind me."

I thought of all the troubled times in class when I'd caught Reggie's eye and she'd winked at me. Yep, it sure helps to know a friend is behind you. I felt like a monster: half chicken and half rat. "I honestly can't make up my mind," I whined.

"Coward," Reggie replied, more disappointed than angry.

"Have I ever denied it?"

The class looked weird, all in white shirts and dark skirts and trousers. The Christmas program's official uniform. You could tell everyone felt weird, too, because there was a lot of extra giggling going on. For the moment, nobody paid any attention to me, thank goodness.

I slithered into my seat. Forty-five minutes until the program. About forty-seven minutes until my decision would be made, one way or the other. Suddenly, my mind went completely blank, clicked right off. My head felt empty, as if my brain had fallen out. Terrified, I stared at my desk. I could see the heart scratched into it, with its tender inscription: "Me and joani, true love, yeah." I wondered if I still knew how to read it. Then I realized I had already read it, so my brain had to be working. Part time, anyway.

The light in the room seemed brighter than usual, super bright. Apparently my eyes were out of order, too. Terrific. Maybe I'd disintegrate, one bodily part at a time. In forty-seven minutes, there'd be nothing left of me but a little heap of clothing and memories. Only now it was forty-three minutes.

And then it was five minutes and we were lining up. I refused to look at Terry or Reggie, even when Reggie handed me my candle. I knew it was Reggie because she had her sparkly silver Christmas nail polish on her six good nails. The bitten nails weren't allowed to wear polish. I don't know who lighted my candle. I didn't look up. Frantic, I tried to give all my attention to the little flickering flames. How could I let down my friends? I couldn't. How could I make such a spectacle of myself? I couldn't. I wouldn't make any decision at all. I'd leave it to fate. Whatever happened when I got to the middle of that gym would happen.

Mrs. Morton began "Oh, Come, All Ye Faithful," and the line started shuffling toward the gym. My lips and mouth were parched; nothing came out but a crackling sound. I gave up on singing and moved my mouth as best as I could, but it soon went numb. Butterflies danced the Virginia reel in my stomach.

I turned the corner into the gym. The bleachers to my left were packed with parents and little brothers and sisters. My neck was frozen stiff, so I had to peek out of the corner of my eye. It looked like a huge wall of waving colors and shapes. I was halfway to the center of the gym when I heard Terry's voice pipe out: "We want Mrs. Morton. We want Mrs. Morton." He sounded like such a little kid, I almost laughed.

Then a murmur swelled up from the audience. I could hardly hear Reggie when she joined Terry, there was such a hubbub. The person ahead of me faltered for a second. My candle practically set fire to her hair. Then she turned right and started up the aisle. There was this huge empty space ahead of me, miles and miles of shiny wooden floor, with Terry and Reggie sailing across it ever so slowly, *in slow motion!* How were they doing that? I could hardly see or hear, but everything on my left seemed to be seething. Somebody was yelling and the lights were flashing on and off.

Suddenly, my candle went out. My feet followed Reggie's path and I was croaking, "We want Mrs. Morton. We want Mrs. Morton." How far could it be from the middle of the gym to that door? When I finally got there, I felt as if I'd walked for a month through a lake of glue. Reggie and Terry were jumping for joy. They cracked heads trying to hug me both at once. They laughed and laughed, a regular pair of loons.

"What do we do now?" I asked, shaking so hard I thought my teeth would come unstuck.

"I don't know," Reggie said, her voice suddenly hushed in amazement.

"We didn't plan anything else," Terry admitted.

"Wonderful," I said. "Well, I hope we can get jobs, because we're going to be thrown out of school."

# 10

I dragged myself down the hall, away from the gym. Dr. Kyle was making an announcement, but I didn't want to hear what it was. Eventually I stopped shaking and went totally numb. The halls, Mrs. Morton's room, the desks and chairs, all looked flat. The world and I were quietly collapsing, tidily folding ourselves up so we could tuck ourselves neatly away. But where?

Terry and Reggie came tumbling into the room after me.

"Yahoo!" Terry screamed. "Yahoo! Yahoo!"

Mrs. Morton was the next one in. She quickly closed

the door behind her. "Terry, stop that," she said. "There are reporters out there."

"Reporters!" Reggie squealed.

"Didn't you see the flashbulbs popping all over the gym?" Mrs. Morton asked.

"I didn't see anything," Reggie said.

"Me neither," Terry put in. "I was too scared."

I remembered thinking the lights were flashing on and off, but didn't say anything. I'd already said enough for a lifetime.

A smile played around the corners of Mrs. Morton's mouth. She covered it with a hand that was poking her glasses into place. "I don't know whether to thank you or spank you," she said. "I never thought you'd do it."

That last part was directed at me.

"Me, neither," I said.

The door swung open and Dr. Kyle swooped down on us.

"You three—no, you *four*" he hissed, "are to stay in this room until everyone leaves the building at noon. Is that clear? I will speak with you then." He started back out, but Mrs. Morton stopped him.

"Are we being held prisoner?" she demanded.

"Call it protective custody," Dr. Kyle snapped.

"What about the eighth-grade party?" Mrs. Morton asked. She was very calm now, like the eye of a hurricane.

"What about it?"

"The other children and their parents are due in here after the program. I've got an office full of cupcakes."

"I'll announce that the eighth-grade party will be held

in the gym. If and when we get through the program. You'd better give me the cupcakes. I don't want you out there with those reporters."

Mrs. Morton piled four bakery boxes into his arms, then took one back. "For us," she said, brightly.

Dr. Kyle spun around and practically knocked over a reporter with his cupcakes.

"Dr. Kyle, what do you intend to do about this protest?" the reporter asked. She was trying to shove a tiny microphone over the boxes and into Dr. Kyle's face.

"I have no comment," Dr. Kyle said. Just like on the evening news! I had to admit this mess was getting kind of exciting.

"May I speak to the students involved?" a second reporter wanted to know.

"Absolutely not," Dr. Kyle informed him, butting him out the door with the cupcake boxes.

But the first reporter slipped in. "Mrs. Morton," she asked, "what was your part in the protest?"

"She had nothing to do with it," Terry yelped before Mrs. Morton could answer.

"Then it was your idea?" the reporter asked, immediately aiming her mike at Terry. "What's your name?"

"Please leave this room immediately," Mrs. Morton insisted. The reporter began backing out, talking the whole time.

"Do you plan to go to court? Have you notified your union?"

At the door, a photographer aimed a camera over Dr. Kyle's head.

"Out! Out!" Dr. Kyle barked. The photographer and the reporter who was backing out collided in the doorway and then disappeared. Mrs. Morton slammed the door shut after them. Dr. Kyle's flushed face filled the little glass window in the door.

"You'd better lock this door," Mrs. Morton shouted at him, "or they'll be back the minute you walk away."

"All right," Dr. Kyle agreed, "and then I'm going to call some parents."

"Mine are in New York," Reggie yelled back. "I'm staying with my aunt. We're leaving for New York tomorrow."

"Then I will call your aunt," Dr. Kyle said through clenched teeth. "Now please stay put!" He shot Mrs. Morton a hateful look and vanished. Curious faces immediately filled his place at the window. Mrs. Morton tore off a strip of brown paper and we helped her tape it over the glass.

"Ah!" she said. "Alone at last."

"Oh, wow, this is exciting," Reggie said, breathlessly.

"Oh, wow, isn't it?" Mrs. Morton echoed with a chuckle. But she didn't sound all that thrilled.

She sat on her desk and the three of us took our seats. It was funny. Even with nobody else there, we sat in our regular seats.

"Well, here we are," Mrs. Morton said. "What shall we do?"

We all looked at each other and shrugged.

"We could sing the Christmas program," Mrs. Morton suggested. "It would pass the time."

We groaned.

"I've got a question," Terry said.

"Yes?"

"Why didn't you ever mention you were Jewish? Before that note, I mean? Like when Summer first showed you the editorial? Or all the time we were rehearsing for the Christmas program."

"First of all, no one ever asked me. And second of all, I don't believe a teacher's religion should be used to influence a class."

"But how do you feel about the Christmas program?" Reggie wondered.

"Quite frankly, now that so much has been said and done, I am relieved to make my feelings about it known: I agree with everything Summer said in her editorial."

"Did you ever complain to Dr. Kyle?" Terry asked.

"No. And I can also admit now that I'm ashamed of that. I simply lacked the courage. You may not believe it, but a teacher often learns more from her students than the other way around."

We were all quiet for a while. I was thinking how terrific Mrs. Morton was. How many adults will admit they learn stuff from children? I don't mean how to play Monopoly. I mean important stuff, like courage. Then I started to get choked up, because I remembered Mrs. Morton was leaving.

"Tell us about Hanukkah," Terry suggested.

"Yes, teach us a Hanukkah song. Maybe we can sneak it in next year," Reggie said.

"Oh, my goodness," Mrs. Morton laughed, "a Hanukkah song. Well, it's been a long time for me. Let me think." She looked toward the window for a moment, and then continued. "The only one I can remember is a little children's song. It's called, 'I Have a Little Dreidel.'"

"What's a dreidel?" Terry asked.

"I know," Reggie said. "It's like a little spinning top. It has Hebrew letters on four sides and you spin it, and depending on which side it lands on, you get some nuts or you lose some."

"Very good," Mrs. Morton said. "Where did you learn that?"

"Oh, my grandparents in New York live in a Jewish neighborhood. When we go there to celebrate Christmas, everybody else in the apartment building is celebrating Hanukkah!"

"Well, the song goes like this:

> I have a little dreidel,
> I made it out of clay,
> And when it is all finished
> Then dreidel I will play . . ."

Reggie started to giggle first, I think. Mrs. Morton really doesn't have a very good voice. Laughing doesn't help it, either. By the end of the last chorus, we were roaring, Mrs. Morton included. But we were clapping our hands, too, and singing along at the top of our lungs:

> "Oh, dreidel, dreidel, dreidel,
> I made it out of clay.

Oh, dreidel, dreidel, dreidel,
Then dreidel I will play."

We finished up with a big round of applause and a "Bravo!" from Terry. Mrs. Morton took a few bows. Then she got serious.

"You have to remember," she said, "that Hanukkah isn't as important a holiday to Jews as Christmas is to Christians. It's more of a fun kind of holiday, with presents for children and games and songs. It gets a lot of publicity, though, because it falls so close to Christmas and a lot of people think it's the Jewish Christmas, which it isn't."

"What is?" Reggie wanted to know.

"Nothing. We don't celebrate any kind of Christmas because Jesus Christ isn't part of our religion. That's hard for you to picture, I guess, but that's the way it is. Our really big holidays are Rosh Hashanah, which comes in the fall and is our new year. And Yom Kippur, which comes ten days later. But I really don't want to give a lecture on Judaism. There are books in the library, you know, if you're interested."

"Somebody ought to teach all that," Terry said. "And about Hindu and Buddhism and all the other religions."

Mrs. Morton turned away quickly and we remembered she wasn't going to be teaching us anything anymore.

To change the subject, Reggie asked, "What do those little Hebrew letters on the dreidels mean, Mrs. Morton? I used to know, but I've forgotten."

Mrs. Morton brushed a hand across one cheek and

**85**

cleared her throat. "Oh, well, the four letters are the beginning of four Hebrew words. I've forgotten the Hebrew, but it means "A great miracle happened there."

"Where?"

"In the Holy Land. Actually, in Israel, dreidels have a different letter on them because they have to say "A great miracle happened *here*."

"What was the miracle?" Reggie wondered.

Mrs. Morton was quiet for a moment. "Come to think of it," she said, at last, "it's rather appropriate. Very briefly, a long time ago, the Syrians decided the local Jews should give up their religion and worship as the Syrians did. A small band of Jews, called the Maccabees, led a successful battle against the Syrians. But when the Jews returned to their temple they found it had been badly wrecked and that they had very little oil left for the Eternal Light. The Eternal Light is supposed to burn continually in the temple—sort of representing God's presence. Well, they had only enough oil for one day. But the light went on burning for eight days, until they could get more oil. That was the miracle. And that's why we light candles for eight days at Hanukkah time. Hanukkah is also known as the Festival of Lights. Anyway, that battle was the first known fight for religious freedom. And, as you know, it wasn't the last."

We were very quiet. To think, I was part of something that went back thousands of years. It was really remarkable.

"Let's break out the refreshments," Mrs. Morton decided. We tackled our box of cupcakes with a vengeance. There were a dozen. We were so hungry, we each gobbled down three in no time at all. Then we found we were dying of thirst.

"We ought to bang our tin cups against the bars of our cell," Terry said.

"We don't have tin cups," I reminded him. "Or bars."

"I've got coffee in my thermos," Mrs. Morton offered. "Milk, no sugar."

"Fine with me," Terry said.

"Me, too," Reggie added.

I don't like coffee very much. But if Mrs. Morton had offered dirty dishwater, I wouldn't have turned it down. One, because I was so thirsty, and two, because it was hers.

We raised our styrofoam cups and toasted each other.

"To religious freedom," Terry added, after we'd all been saluted.

"To freedom of the press," Mrs. Morton added.

"To *freedom*," Reggie and I said together. We laughed and drank up.

# 11

It was past noon. We heard chattering and laughter in the hall. Terry peeked under an edge of the brown paper.

"Everyone's leaving," he said. University School lets out at noon before Christmas vacation. Except for the seniors, who stay to rehearse their play for that night. Suddenly, Terry flipped the paper back into place. "Peekers," he explained.

"Well," Mrs. Morton said, "we should be set free any minute now.

That sounded good to me. The coffee was beginning to affect me. I wondered if anybody else had to go to the bathroom. Nobody mentioned it.

Another forty-five anxious minutes went by. The halls were eerily quiet. Mrs. Morton peeled away the brown paper and we all peered out, pressing our cheeks against the glass to see as far in both directions as we could. Everything was still.

"You don't suppose he forgot about us?" Reggie asked.

"I can see it all now," Terry said, "January 2. Headline: Janitor Discovers Four Corpses."

"Honestly," Reggie said, "sometimes I think you have newsprint where your brain ought to be."

We cleaned up our paper cups and crumbs and waited some more. When the footsteps finally came, they took me by surprise. I'd been lost in thought, redesigning the classroom to contain a toilet. We all looked at each other and shared weak smiles of encouragement.

"Here we go," Terry murmured.

Dr. Kyle unlocked the door and came in, followed by Dad and another man who was short, chunky, and totally bald.

"Dr. Transkill, have you met Mrs. Morton?" Dr. Kyle asked.

My stomach flip-flapped as Mrs. Morton shook hands with Dr. Transkill. I forgot all about designing toilets. I'd never seen Dr. Transkill before. I expected him to stand at least seven feet tall and maybe even to breathe fire. But he looked very ordinary. Dad shook Mrs. Morton's hand, too, and then came and sat on my desk.

"Political prisoner, hey?" he whispered out of the side of his mouth. I tried to smile up at him, but my face was stuck.

Dr. Transkill sat down on another desk and so did Dr. Kyle. Dr. Kyle let his eyes wander over the room. He looked older somehow, tired and kind of sad.

"Another semester tucked away," he sighed, speaking to no one in particular.

Feet shuffled. Terry coughed. We waited.

Finally, Dr. Kyle spoke again.

"I couldn't reach your father, Terry. Or your aunt, Regina," he said. Reggie's full name sounded weird. She hates it. Once, in fifth grade, Murray Hamm called her "vagina." She grabbed his hair in both hands and threatened to leave him bald if he ever said that to her again. He never did.

"I'm very grateful that you could be here, Dr. Transkill," Dr. Kyle went on. "You, too, Dr. Smith. I know you're both very busy men."

"No problem," Dad said, pleasantly. Dr. Transkill nodded in agreement.

"I wish I could say the same," Dr. Kyle told them. "But we have quite a problem here. I appreciate your interest in settling it."

We four culprits shifted in our seats. I glanced at Mrs. Morton. She seemed to be examining the back of her right hand very carefully, running her left thumb back and forth on it.

"What we have here," Dr. Kyle continued, "is a complete disregard for appropriate school behavior."

"I don't think so," Dad said.

All eyes turned toward him.

"I think these children have had a tremendous learning

90

experience. That's what school is all about, isn't it?"

"These children," Dr. Kyle said, "have disrupted an entire week of classes. I don't call that a tremendous learning experience."

"It's not as if they'd disrupted classes by twiddling their thumbs," Dad insisted. I heard Reggie choke back a nervous giggle. "They put out a newspaper, which is a valuable experience in itself. They've been harassed for their beliefs, which is another valuable experience, however painful. And they've defended their beliefs, realizing in the process the challenges and responsibilities of freedom. All in all, I'd say they've had an enormously educational week."

I love to hear Dad speak like that. He makes the English language sound as if it came on gold leaf. But Dr. Kyle wasn't impressed.

"At the expense of everyone else," he snapped. "Their beliefs, as you call them, have caused fights among children, parents, and teachers, and disrupted our traditional Christmas program. In front of reporters, I might add, reporters who will be happy to use *their* freedom of the press to ruin the reputation of this school."

Dr. Transkill cleared his throat. "Exactly what kind of fighting among the children, parents, and teachers has been going on?" he asked Dr. Kyle.

"A fistfight between the Chong twins and some of their classmates. Some teasing of the Caplan girl by a group of third graders. Mrs. Caplan has been to school every day this week complaining about that editorial. And she's *Jewish*."

"We got one rather foolish but nasty phone call," Dad added.

"And there was a—a note directed at Summer and me," Mrs. Morton put in.

"Anything else?" Dr. Transkill wanted to know.

"Well," Dr. Kyle went on, "there was considerable confusion caused by this . . . ah . . . protest demonstration during the Christmas program. It was all I could do to get the program back in order again."

"But you did."

"Eventually, yes. I believe a good deal of the spirit of the thing was lost, but we got through it."

"And that's all?" Dr. Transkill asked.

"All?" Dr. Kyle echoed in disbelief. "All?"

"Yes. All. Is there anything else?"

"Isn't this enough?" Dr. Kyle asked. "Oh, and of course, this protest will be in tonight's paper. With photographs, I imagine."

Dr. Transkill nodded gravely. Then he stood up and began pacing slowly around the room. We all watched him, holding our breath. He fingered the book-jacket display on one bulletin board thoughtfully, poked at the plants on the windowsill, then gazed out the window, whistling something unrecognizable. At last, he turned back to us.

"Not only will it be in tonight's paper," he said, "but there will be a follow-up article, I'm sure. The public will want to know how we handled this situation. As I see it, we have two choices. We could discipline these children, indicating that we disapprove of their actions. This would

92

satisfy a few people, perhaps, but it would mean coming out against freedom of the press—well, freedom of expression in general, I would say. On the other hand, we could support the children, expressing our belief that what they did was a valid part of the educational process, and of the democratic process. And, by so doing, we'd make those same few people angry."

"Very," Dr. Kyle agreed.

"In my opinion," Dr. Transkill went on, "there is really only one choice: the second."

"I agree," Dad said.

Dr. Kyle's mouth opened and shut with a snap.

Mrs. Morton beamed at Dr. Transkill. Her glasses slipped down her nose. She pushed them back up and went on beaming.

"Mrs. Morton, is your resignation official at this point?" Dr. Transkill wanted to know.

"Well, I haven't signed anything yet, if that's what you mean. It's not in writing."

"Good. Then I hope you can be persuaded to stay on here, now that your point of view has been understood as being in the true interests of this school."

"Well, I . . ." Mrs. Morton began, blushing.

"Oh, please, Mrs. Morton, *please!*" Terry and Reggie and I begged, jumping up to surround her.

"I don't know," she finished, looking at Dr. Kyle.

Dr. Kyle ran a hand through his fringe, making it stand out as if he'd been electrocuted.

"Really, this is going to make me look like a fool," he muttered.

"It's been a difficult week," Dr. Transkill told him. "The end of the semester is always difficult. And the actions of this class magnified the difficulties a hundred-fold. We all understand that, Dr. Kyle. And if you erred a bit in your judgment, I think we will all have no problem forgiving you."

Dr. Kyle shot Dr. Transkill an odd look, as if forgiveness was not what he'd expected. "And what about the Chongs and Mrs. Caplan?" he asked.

"I will personally speak to both families," Dr. Transkill said. "I'm sorry they were made to suffer, but when a truth emerges—as it did in Ms. Smith's editorial—everything shifts and, unfortunately, minority groups are often bruised in the process. In the long run, though, the truth is in their favor. I'll try to convince them of that."

*Ms.* Smith's editorial! I really liked that!

"And the crank callers and the nasty note writers?"

"I like Dr. Transkill's image of the truth emerging and everything shifting," Dad responded. "When a rock shifts, all sorts of slimy things are uncovered, aren't they? But given no encouragement, they quickly hide themselves again."

"And perhaps with that rock out of the way," Dr. Transkill added, "some healthy things can begin to grow."

Mrs. Morton laughed then. And Dad's eyes twinkled.

"We are waxing poetical, aren't we?" he said.

"The point is," Dr. Transkill said, addressing Dr. Kyle, "do we run this school to please others or to educate our children?"

Dr. Kyle's face blotched red and purple.

94

"I know," Dr. Transkill went on, "that it is sometimes run to please Transkills. Very flattering, but not always in the children's best interests."

Dr. Kyle nodded. He and Dr. Transkill exchanged a long look. Dr. Kyle seemed less old and tired, suddenly. He turned to Mrs. Morton. "Will you accept my apology and stay on?" he asked.

"Yes, sir, I will," Mrs. Morton replied, her head high.

Reggie squealed joyously. Terry and I grinned.

"Children," Dr. Transkill said, "I think your work has already accomplished a great deal of good by opening lines of communication between Dr. Kyle and Mrs. Morton and myself."

"Thank you, sir," Terry spoke out, for all of us.

"Dr. Kyle," Dad put in, "I can speak from experience when I assure you the worst of this will pass sooner than you think. People forget quickly."

"I suppose you're right," Dr. Kyle admitted.

"Until next Christmas anyway," Dad added, with a twinkle.

"Well, that gives you an entire year to plan a more satisfactory program," Dr. Transkill said. Again, Dr. Kyle's mouth fell open. "Traditions are very nice," Dr. Transkill went on, "but they have to grow and change along with everything else. I had great respect for my grandfather, Dr. Kyle, but I don't travel in his horse and buggy."

There was a lot of handshaking and laughter after that. In the midst of it, I remembered something I'd completely forgotten. It seemed as if the handshaking and farewells were going to take forever. I smiled and smiled, but my teeth ached and my eyes were starting to water.

"Will we see you at the senior play tonight, Dr. Transkill?" Mrs. Morton asked. She and Dr. Transkill were blocking the doorway.

"Never miss it," Dr. Transkill assured her.

And then he was gone. The coast was clear. I flew down the hall and into the ladies' room.

# 12

I thought I was finished with The Press at last. I was happy to leave it to Woodward and Bernstein and Terry.

But The Press wasn't finished with me.

Oh, there was one nice thing, a letter that appeared in the evening paper. This is what is said:

Dear Editor,

In regard to the episode at University School, it is written, "And a child shall lead them." The question remains: Will they follow?

Yours sincerely,
A Christian for Brotherhood

"Your first fan letter," Dad said, handing me the paper.

It made me feel good, but not good enough, because things immediately started rolling downhill.

We were ready to leave for the senior play when the phone rang.

"It's Douglas!" I shouted, hearing my brother's cheerful "Hey, Summer" on the other end of the line. "Hey, Douglas," I cried, "how are you? Are you coming home for Christmas? What's up?"

"No, I'm not coming home, kiddo. I've got a job for winter break. What's up, though, is *you*. You made the paper out here!"

"What?"

"Uh-huh, it's a wire-service article. It says someone by the name of Summer Smith wrote an editorial and got a teacher fired and disrupted a Christmas pageant with a protest march involving a handful of students. How did you get all those students in your hand?"

"Oh, Douglas, they weren't in my hand. Besides, there were just three of us: me and Terry and Reggie. And we didn't get Mrs. Morton fired. She quit. But she's back anyway."

"Well, it goes to show you: You can't believe everything you see in print. They did get your name right, didn't they? You are the Summer Smith they mean?"

"Yes, it's me."

"You must really be growing up. It's not like the Summer I knew to write editorials and stage protests."

"No, it's not. And I'm glad it's over."

"I don't know. National recognition. You may have to run for President next."

"Oh, Douglas," I giggled. Then I noticed Mother and Dad standing there, grimacing and waving their hands and pointing to their ears. "I think Mother and Dad want to talk to you," I told Douglas.

"Well, okay, but I wanted to tell you I'm proud of you, Summer. Seriously."

"Thanks, Douglas," I said, suddenly very shy. "I'm proud of you, too." Douglas laughed. I guess that did sound kind of silly, but I didn't know what else to say. Douglas made a kissing sound and I made one back. Douglas is the big kisser in our family. When he's not around, kisses become an endangered species.

I handed the phone over to Mother. Dad dashed upstairs to the extension. They talked for a while, mostly about Douglas' job and whether he needed anything. Then they hung up. Dad started down the stairs and the phone rang again.

"I'll get it," Mother told him.

Dad and I stood in the hall, bundling into our coats and hats and listening to Mother's side of the conversation.

"Yes, I see . . . No, I don't think so . . . No, I'd really rather not . . . Well, thank you . . . Yes, but . . . I am sorry, but I think not . . . Good-bye."

"Who was that?" Dad asked. "A magazine salesman?"

"No," Mother answered, "a magazine reporter." She looked at me oddly, as if trying to figure out who this annoying little creature could be. "He wanted to do an article on America's Mermaid at middle age." She whipped her coat around her and stomped outside. Dad and I followed.

"When the truth emerges, everything shifts," I heard

him mutter. The phone was ringing again. Dad pulled the door shut and locked it behind us.

Mother sat very stiffly beside Dad on the way to school. I huddled in the back seat with that sick feeling I get whenever she's angry. I don't even know what the crime is, but I feel guilty. None of us spoke.

It was a relief to bump into Reggie at the front door. We begged to sit together, and her aunt and Dad finally let us go off by ourselves. There weren't enough seats for all five of us to sit together.

"What part do you think Rod will have?" Reggie whispered. "The lead, I bet. The romantic lead. What else?"

"How about the basketball player?" I suggested.

"The basketball player? There's no basketball player in *Oklahoma!*"

The juniors were serving as ushers. A skinny girl with braces on her teeth led us to two seats in the second row but way over to the left.

"Oooh, we're really close," Reggie squealed.

"Kind of sideways," I said. It was a good seat, though, for looking around at everybody else in the audience. The place was packed. Everything smelled like wet wool. People were waving and yelling "Hi!" across the rows. We saw Terry come in and waved frantically, but he didn't see us. Reggie's aunt and my parents were in the center section, in one of the last rows. Mother was smiling, but not toward us. I craned my head all the way around, and whom should I find seated two rows behind us but Marjory Warren. She glared at me haughtily and I spun my head back into place.

"Marjory Warren," I told Reggie between my teeth. "Two rows back with her family."

Reggie started to turn around.

"Don't look now!" I warned her.

"Oh, what's to look at?" Reggie said. "I'd be happy to spend my entire life without ever looking at her."

Nevertheless, she took the first opportunity to give Marjory a nasty glance. But when she turned back again, she looked as if she'd seen a ghost.

"What's wrong?" I asked.

"It's Rod," she whispered. "He's back there in the audience."

Now it was my turn to steal a look. Reggie grabbed my arm. With the hand that had all its nails.

"Don't! Don't! Don't!" she pleaded.

"Okay, okay, okay," I said. "Get your claws out of my arm."

"What's he doing out here?" Reggie wondered. "Why isn't he backstage?"

"Maybe he doesn't come on until later."

"Yeah. Or maybe he enters from the audience." Very casually, Reggie let her eyes sweep over the audience, taking Rod in in the process.

"He's not in costume," she reported.

"He probably has plenty of time."

"But why's he sitting in the middle of a row? If he has to go change, you'd think he'd be sitting on the aisle."

The lights dimmed. Three musicians took their places at the side of the stage: a pianist, a violinist, and a drummer. Everyone applauded their entrance. Mr. Wilderman, our music teacher, followed them in.

"Shhhhh," I told Reggie. "It's beginning."

Actually, the violinist was just tuning up.

"I don't understand it," Reggie muttered beside me in the dark.

The violinist finished tuning. Mr. Wilderman raised his baton and the overture began.

"Maybe he's not in the play!" Reggie went on. "Is that possible? I thought all the seniors were in the play."

"Maybe he tried out and didn't make it."

"Rod? Are you crazy?"

"Shhhhh," somebody behind us hissed. Probably Marjory Warren.

Reggie slumped low in her seat. I glanced over and saw she was biting her nails. I pushed her hand away, but she grunted and put it back.

The first act was pretty good. The girl playing Ado Annie was very funny. Everybody else was okay. Cindy Grant had the lead, of course. She almost forgot her lines twice, but she got them out, finally. I didn't know the guy playing opposite her. His voice kept cracking on the high notes.

We spent the intermission spying on the audience from our seats. Mostly spying on Rod, who sat there looking kind of blue. Reggie's eyes filled up just from watching him.

"What if Cindy really falls in love with that guy playing Curly?" she said. "What if she leaves Rod?"

"So much the better for you," I told her.

"But he looks so sad."

"Maybe it's indigestion."

102

She threw me a dirty look and continued spying over the back of her seat. Marjory had gone out into the hall, so we had a clear view.

The second act was a lot worse than the first. I guess they hadn't rehearsed it as much. Curly got the giggles at one point and couldn't say his lines. Cindy looked angry enough to bite off his nose. But they got through it, finally, and the audience applauded and cheered as if it had been terrific.

As soon as the curtain fell, Reggie wanted to push up the aisle to where Rod was, but we couldn't. Something or somebody was holding up traffic and we were crammed in the aisle, waiting for the mob ahead of us to move on.

"Mooooo-ooooo," somebody bellowed. Everybody laughed.

Slowly, we inched our way up to the doors. Then Dad yanked me out of the crowd by my elbow.

"Good night, Reggie," he said abruptly.

"Night, Reggie," I called as he hustled me up the hall. "Call me!"

"I'm going to New York tomorrow," she called back.

"Oh, that's right. Have a great time!"

"Thanks. Take care of your neighbors!"

I waved an okay sign. By then Dad and I were at the end of the hall.

"Where's Mother?" I asked.

"In the ladies' room. Tell her it's safe to come out."

"What?"

"A reporter and a photographer ambushed her on our way up the aisle. Suddenly, she's hot news again."

"Because of me?" I said.

"I guess so. Now, go rescue her, okay?"

I opened the ladies' room door and went in. It looked strange, so empty and clean. During the day, it was usually filled with high-school girls grabbing a quick smoke. Even the trash cans looked odd, without paper towels pouring over their brims.

Mother was fixing her lipstick at one of the mirrors.

"Dad says it's safe to come out now," I said.

"Thank you," she replied, not looking at me.

"I'm sorry about all this."

She glanced my way, but didn't say anything. I started out and, after a moment, she followed.

More silence on the way home. Except for "Good night," the silence continued until I went up to bed. Then everything exploded.

"I really don't see why you're acting this way," Dad began.

"You don't? Well, how would you like to be reminded, publicly, coast-to-coast, that you're a middle-aged has-been?"

"You're not a middle-aged has-been."

"Oh, no? Then what did that reporter mean by 'Whatever happened to America's Mermaid?'"

"She grew up and got married and had a family and a career in education. What's so bad about that?"

It was very faint, but I could hear Mother crying. I bit my lip and soon was crying right along with her. They must have gone into the kitchen then because I didn't hear any more. Eventually, I fell asleep and dreamed about being buried alive. I woke up in the middle of the night, soaked with cold sweat. Groggily, I changed my pajamas and crawled back into bed. I tried to stay awake because I didn't want to dream anymore, but I dozed off and dreamed the same dream all over again.

# 13

I got down to the kitchen first and was nibbling some toast when Mother appeared. She must have had a rough night, too, because her eyes were red and swollen.

"Good morning," I offered, cautiously.

"Morning," she said, and busied herself with the coffeepot.

"I think I'll do some Christmas shopping this morning," I told her.

"All right."

With that, I finished my toast and escaped back to my room. I dawdled away the hour or so until the stores opened, then dashed outside to catch the bus. I could have walked to the mall, but it was really cold and windy.

At first, I didn't recognize the figure hunched against the wind at the bus stop. It looked like a stuffed man, a scarecrow bundled into a coat, earmuffs, and scarf. The closer I got, the taller the scarecrow grew. Then I realized it was Rod Whitman.

We said hi, muffled by our scarves. It wasn't possible to talk in that wind, but I kept thinking I ought to be saying something clever and fascinating. I was very grateful when the bus finally swung into view. Rod let me on first and then slipped into the seat beside me. That really surprised me, because there were plenty of other seats. We pulled down our scarves and said hi again. I began taking mental notes to report to Reggie.

"What are you doing out so early?" Rod asked.

I shrugged. "I was awake, so I thought I might as well get my shopping done."

"Me, too," he nodded. There was a very awkward pause and then he said, "Summer."

"What?" I nearly jumped out of my seat. My name in his voice sounded really weird.

"I was just saying, Summer. Your name reminded me that I wish it *were* summer. This must be the worst winter since the Ice Age."

"I guess so," I agreed.

"How did you get a name like Summer?" Rod asked.

"Oh, well, my mother swims, you know. I guess summer was her favorite time of the year." I wished I would stop saying "I guess" with every sentence I uttered.

"That makes you her favorite person then, huh?"

"Hmmmm," I mused, "I gue . . . I think between the season and the person, she probably prefers the season."

Rod looked surprised, but he didn't say anything. The bus pulled up in front of the mall entrance. I was relieved to let go of that conversation. Rod got off first and put out a hand to help me down the steps and over a hill of shoveled snow. I think I was more nervous about taking his hand than about falling on my face. Worst of all would be taking his hand *and* falling on my face. But there didn't seem to be any alternative, so I put my mitten out and hoped for the best. He must be strong as an ox, because I sailed over that heap of snow and landed safely on the sidewalk before I could think twice about it.

The minute I hit ground, I took my hand back. Rod was already holding the door to the mall open. I looked around to see who he was holding it for. For whom he was holding it. In that instant, about eight people from the bus filed on through. Rod still stood there, expectantly, so I went through, too.

"Maybe I could get a part-time job as doorman," he said, grinning. He pulled off his earmuffs and scarf. He really does have beautiful blond hair, I thought. Reggie was right about that. I looked away quickly, my cheeks flaming. I hoped he would think it was because of the cold.

"What are you shopping for?" he asked.

"A gift for my dad," I told him. My Christmas fund was back up to eight dollars now, thanks to the snow.

"Oh, well, I need to get a going-away present for

Cindy. Cindy Grant. I guess we're headed in different directions."

"Where's she going?"

"To Chicago. She has relatives there. She'll be gone the whole vacation."

"That's too bad."

"Yeah." He didn't sound brokenhearted. I wondered why not, but I didn't say anything.

"Listen, why don't we meet at the doughnut shop in an hour or so? I'll treat you to a hot chocolate and then we can take the bus home together."

"Oh, you don't have to do that," I said.

"I know. But I'm feeling generous."

"Well, okay."

"See you in an hour, then." I watched him move away through the crowd. He was about a head taller than anyone else there.

Oh, why was Reggie in New York at a time like this? It could have been the biggest day of her entire life. I could also have used her there to help carry on the conversation. What in the world did I have to say to Rod Whitman that could last through an entire cup of hot chocolate?

The tiny, crowded Dunky Donut shop tables left me no place to put my packages. I had to balance them on my knees with one hand while I maneuvered my hot chocolate with the other. One large package might have been manageable, but two small ones kept slipping every which way. I was dying for a jelly doughnut, but I didn't order one. I didn't want my face dripping crumbs and jelly in front of Rod.

In between every two sips of hot chocolate, I dabbed my mouth with a napkin so I wouldn't drool. Rod cheerfully arranged three chocolate-cream-filled crullers and a huge glass of milk in front of himself and proceeded to stuff it all in. Watching him, I prayed that hot chocolate would be enough to keep my stomach from growling.

While shopping for Dad's gift, I'd made a mental list of questions I could ask Rod to keep the conversation going. Reggie owns several books on getting along with the opposite sex, and they all suggest asking the other person questions about himself. Rod must have read those books, too, because he started right in by asking what I'd bought. I told him a key case and a tie for Dad. He told me he'd found a charm for Cindy's charm bracelet and asked if I wanted to see it. Before I could say anything (I was thinking No), he'd whipped it out. It was a tiny silver megaphone. I admired it about as much as you can admire a tiny silver megaphone without sounding phony. In my opinion, he *should* have been shopping for *Reggie*—and buying her an enormous golden heart.

For a while after that, we gave a lot of attention to our snacks. I dabbed my lips as usual and waited for Rod's next question. It never came, so I figured it must be my turn.

"How come you weren't in the senior play?" I asked.

*Wrong question.*

Rod looked as if a "tilt" sign were going to light up on his forehead. With great care, he flipped a lone doughnut crumb along the tabletop. "I . . . uh . . . oh, I don't know," he said. "I just wasn't, I guess."

I nodded as if I understood exactly what he meant,

which I didn't, of course. Then I dropped the subject and moved right on to my next question.

"When's your next basketball game?"

That was better. He shoved the end of his third doughnut into his mouth and thought about that for a minute.

"January the third," he said. "Roxbury, at home. Should be a good game. Do you go to the games?"

I had to admit I didn't. "I'm not very sports-minded," I explained.

"With a mom who's an Olympic champ? That's surprising."

A *mom?* I thought. I never called her that.

"I guess I take after my dad. We exercise by rapidly turning pages in books."

Rod tossed his head back and laughed. "That's very funny," he said.

"Thanks. It's my dad's joke. Mother's always trying to get us to exercise more. Dad says anything that hurts so much can't be good for you."

We smiled about that for a while. Then it got very quiet again. I could've sworn I had one more question on my mental list, but I couldn't remember it.

Suddenly, Rod leaned toward me with a very serious expression on his face. "Summer," he said, "I really admire what you did in school."

"What?" I asked, thinking I'd have to tell Reggie that his eyes were more hazel than blue.

"You know, that editorial and the protest. That took a lot of guts."

"Oh, no, it didn't."

"Oh, yes, it did."

"No, no, it was all a mistake, really. I thought I was writing a nice quiet editorial, and all of a sudden everything blew up around me. All I did was stand there in the middle of it."

"You're just being modest. Everybody saw what you did. You weren't just standing there."

"Well, I didn't have much choice. I mean, if I could have run away, believe me, I would have."

"No, you wouldn't."

"Oh, yes, I would. I can't stand stuff like that—everybody making such a fuss over me. I get terrified."

"You didn't look terrified."

"Well, I was. During the protest, I was—wow, I was in outer space. I didn't even know I was going to do it until I was actually doing it."

"I can't believe that. It all looked so organized."

I had to laugh at that. "Are you kidding? Do you know, when I got to that exit, none of us had the slightest idea of what to do next? I mean, I said to Terry, 'What do we do now?' And he said, 'I don't know. We didn't plan anything else.'"

Rod chuckled. He had a really nice chuckle. A lot of guys his age can chuckle and make you feel like a real idiot, or that they're thinking something dirty about you. But Rod's chuckle is more like a little kid's chuckle, happy and sort of ticklish.

"Well, you looked good," he said. "And I really admire you for getting out there and standing up for what you believe in."

112

My cheeks glowed hotter than the steam from my cup.

"Oh, well, thanks," I said. For some reason, he was going to believe I was Joan of Arc no matter what I said. Didn't he know a Cowardly Lion when he saw one? "But you get out there in front of everybody all the time," I added, "on the basketball court."

Rod looked away. Had I said something wrong?

"Basketball's different," he murmured.

"Well, any kind of getting out there upsets me," I admitted. "I really admire you, too. Even if I've never been to a game."

"Why don't you come on the third?" he asked.

"Oh, wow, I don't know . . ."

"We'll go out afterward for a bite to eat."

Was Rod Whitman asking me for a date? Was my very first date in the entire world going to be with Rod Whitman? There had to be some mistake.

"I'm sorry I can't pick you up before the game," he continued, "but I've got to be there a lot earlier than you need to. Do you think you can get a ride over?"

"Well, I could walk, couldn't I?" I said, from inside what felt like a cloud of cotton candy.

Rod laughed. "Sure, you can walk. Unless there's a blizzard."

"Oh, well, I guess my dad could bring me."

"Okay. Then it's a date. Seven thirty, January third. Let's go catch the bus, huh?"

It's a date. That's what he said. It's a date! Oh, my God, I thought, Reggie is going to kill me!

# 14

Christmas was really depressing. We dragged through all the motions, but with Douglas away and Mother still sulking, it was not very merry.

Snow fell for days afterward. I shoveled our walk and several others on the block. I was getting rich and muscular and bored. Reggie sent a Statue of Liberty postcard. She was having a terrific time. (Reggie, I mean, not the statue.) She told me not to write back because she'd be traveling from one relative's house to the next and I'd probably miss her. That was okay with me. Heaven knows what I'd have written.

I hadn't even told my parents yet about my upcoming

date with Rod. I kept thinking he'd probably call and cancel it, once he'd had time to think it over. Wednesday after Christmas, the phone rang and Mother announced it was for me. Handing me the receiver, she gave me that odd look of hers, as if she'd forgotten I existed and yet here I was, popping in from Planet X to take my call.

It was Rod. "How ya doin'?" came his pleasant voice.

"Okay," I said. Brilliant response. "How are you?" I remembered to add.

"Fine. But I've got a problem."

Oh, sure, I thought. Fire away. He *was* going to cancel our date! Was I disappointed or relieved? A dash of both.

"I have to do this critical review of Bernard Malamud for English class. I was wondering if your dad had any information I might borrow."

"Oh!" I said. Doubly brilliant. Brilliant and *witty*. "Wait a minute. I'll ask him."

I was back to the phone in a flash, having convinced Dad that denying Rod Whitman would be like burning the University School flag.

"Dad says he has some stuff in his files here in the house. But he'd rather you used them here than take them home. Is that okay?"

"Oh, sure. Thanks. Tell him thanks for me."

Dad brushed by just then. "Rod says thanks," I told him.

"Tell him he's welcome, but to come later this afternoon."

"He says you're welcome, but come later this afternoon."

"When?" Rod wanted to know.

"When?" I asked Dad.

"Four. I'll be going out then."

"Four, Rod?"

"Four it is. Thanks again, Summer. See you then."

"Okay. 'Bye."

Four o'clock. That gave me two hours to become human. I was a wreck from shoveling snow and generally hanging around and being messy. I made a beeline for the tub.

Promptly at four o'clock, Rod appeared at our front door. Mother greeted him with one of her best photogenic smiles, then disappeared upstairs. Dad showed him to the files and explained where he might find what he needed. I stood there, freshly clothed and shampooed and useless. Rod spent an hour and a half going through Dad's materials. I sat on the sofa and watched for a while, but it quickly became obvious that he wasn't here for a chat. I'd even thought up lots of new questions to keep the conversational ball rolling. Unfortunately, the ball was deflated.

Why am I doing all this anyway? I asked myself. What's Rod Whitman to me that I should take an extra bath for him? My self refused to answer. It was too busy pouting because Rod had given all his attention to Bernard Malamud. Who would never, I am sure, waste two whole hours primping for Rod Whitman.

Mother came downstairs and started dinner. Despite my numerous messages by mental telepathy, she didn't invite Rod to stay. So, at five thirty-seven, he left, having barely noticed me at all.

116

He did say, "See you on the third," though, and set off a small nuclear war.

"What did he mean by 'See you on the third'?" Mother wanted to know.

I sidled into my seat across from Dad at the dining table. "Well, I've been meaning to talk to you about that," I began.

Two pairs of eyes gave me their undivided attention.

"I happened to meet Rod on the bus going to the mall and . . . well . . . he asked me to come to the basketball game on January third. He said we could go out for something to eat afterward."

"You mean, a date?" Mother asked, her eyes about to pop. Dad twinkled up toward the ceiling.

"I guess so. A little one."

"That boy is a *senior*. What is he, seventeen, eighteen?"

"Seventeen."

"And you are thirteen. No way. Absolutely out of the question."

"Oh, Mother!"

"Angela, maybe . . ." Dad began.

"No maybe about it. She is a thirteen-year-old child. She's never had a date before, and she's not going to start with a seventeen-year-old *man*. What does he want with *you*, anyway?"

That hurt. That really hurt.

"He thinks I'm sexy," I yelled, and bolted up to my room.

"Summer, get back down here."

It was Dad. I immediately felt very foolish about my outburst. There I stood in the middle of my room, huffing and puffing, steam practically pouring out of my ears, and for what? What *did* Rod want with me? What did *I* want with *him*? It was very confusing. I crept back downstairs.

"He doesn't want anything with me," I went on, as if the conversation hadn't been interrupted by my emergency exit. "I told him I'd never been to a game and he said to come next week. That's all. It's only polite to offer someone a bite to eat afterward. Isn't it? Besides, he has a girl friend, Cindy Grant."

"The head cheerleader?" Mother mused, half aloud.

"None other. She's out of town. I guess he's lonely. We got to talking at the mall and he asked me to come to the game."

Dad put away his pipe and attacked his stew. "Sounds harmless enough," he said.

"I'll think about it," Mother announced.

"But, Mother, I already told him yes."

"You had no business telling him yes without checking with us."

"You mean, when a guy asks me for a date, I have to say, 'I'll ask my parents?' I'd *die* before I said that!"

"Angela, maybe you're being unreasonable?"

"I said, I'll think about it."

Another silent dinner. We were getting good at it.

Two more gloomy days passed. The atmosphere was really heavy in our house. The only time it lightened was when Mother went off to the pool for practice sessions with the team.

At night, I heard Mother and Dad hissing back and forth at each other. I knew they were discussing me. I wished I could hear what they were saying. Whatever it was, Dad must have won, because in the end Mother reluctantly agreed that I could go to the game, provided I was home no later than ten thirty.

"The game won't end until after nine," I said. "By the time Rod gets showered and dressed, we won't have time to eat anything."

"Bring him back here," Mother suggested. "We have plenty of food."

"Oh, Mother," I moaned. "He'll think I'm a jerk. A *baby* jerk."

"Most boys his age," Dad put in, "would be grateful not to have to spend their money."

"Oh, okay," I said. It was probably just as well. I had no business going out with Rod anyway. He was Reggie's. Well, actually he was Cindy Grant's, but Reggie was next in line. I'd have to be satisfied with being his friend. Satisfied? I was delirious! There wasn't a gloomy cloud big enough to get my spirits down.

Or so I thought. Little did I know you could rub two small clouds together and make yourself a really major thunderstorm.

The first cloud came in the guise of another call from Douglas. This time Mother and Dad had the extensions. I never even got to say hello. I was up in their bedroom trying to guess Douglas' half of the conversation from Mother's facial expressions. They were not pleasant. When she finally hung up, she looked as if all her blood had been drained away.

"What is it?" I asked. "Did something happen to Douglas?"

Dad came bounding up from the kitchen.

"Now, look," he started in on Mother, "it's not important. It's stupid and cruel, but it's not important."

"What's not important?" I cried. "What's stupid and cruel? Somebody tell me what's going on!"

Dad sat beside Mother on the bed and put his arm around her. She had her head bowed, her forehead on her hand. I couldn't tell if she was crying or what.

After an eternity, Dad noticed me and explained the latest disaster: The reporter and photographer who were hounding Mother had sold a picture and caption to *National Gossip*.

"*National Gossip*? You mean the paper that describes the ax murders and the truth behind the stars' private lives and all that junk?"

"You see," Dad said to the back of Mother's head, "even an eighth grader knows that paper's full of junk."

"What do you mean, *even* an eighth grader?"

Dad shot me a dirty look. It was no time, the look said, to quibble over vocabulary.

"What did they say?" I asked.

"Nothing precise," Dad answered. "They never do. There was a photograph of Mother going into the ladies' room the night of the senior play. And a caption full of innuendos about why she wouldn't grant an interview."

"Middle-age flab," Mother said in a trembly little voice, not lifting her head.

"What?"

"Douglas said the caption suggested that Mother was hiding middle-age flab."

"Mother doesn't have any middle-age flab to hide." It was true. She had a terrific body. She still swam at least an hour a day, five or six days a week.

"Oh, yes, I do," Mother wailed.

Dad stood up. "Really, Angela, I'm not going to baby you through this. You do not have middle-age flab."

"I weigh ten pounds more than I did then."

"Yes, and you're a forty-six-year-old woman. You were a skinny little kid then. It was a wonder I fell in love with you. I could hardly see you."

Now Mother was crying in earnest.

"Oh, go away!" she howled. "Both of you! Get out of here!"

I looked at Dad. He was furious, but he shrugged and gestured toward the door. As we left, he turned to Mother once more. "When you're ready to stop feeling sorry for yourself, let me know."

"If I hadn't written that article . . ." I began, tearfully.

"And the same goes for you!" Dad roared.

I fled into my room.

# 15

The second cloud: Murray Hamm called and invited me to a New Year's Eve party. Of course, I had absolutely no intention of going. First of all, Marjory Warren and her entire clique would be there and Reggie wouldn't. And second of all, drooling over his braces, Murray informed me that the reason he was giving the party was because his parents were going to be out of town. His sister, a junior in high school who wore lavender nail polish, was inviting her friends over, but they would use the upstairs. Murray had the recreation room in the basement.

"Well, listen," he said, after I told him I didn't think I could make it, "whatever you do, you have to swear not to tell *anybody's* parents about these parties. Do you solemnly swear?"

What did it matter to me? I wasn't going anyway. So I swore.

"Who was that?" Mother wanted to know, the minute the receiver clicked down.

"Murray Hamm. The creep who whistles through his braces all the time." Even when he's telling dirty jokes, I thought. *Especially* then.

"What did he want?"

"He's giving a New Year's Eve party and he wanted me to come. I told him I couldn't."

"Why?"

"Because I don't want to go."

"Why not?"

"Because Murray's a creep, and Marjory Warren will be there and she's a creep, and all their friends are creeps. It'll be infested with creeps, like a swamp."

"I think you ought to go."

"Mother!"

"I'd much rather have you go there than have you go out with a seventeen-year-old man."

"Mother, you already said yes to that."

"Well, then, I think you ought to say yes to Murray. If you're going to begin a social life, it ought to be with people your own age."

"Mother, Reggie won't be there. I'll have no one on my side."

123

"Your side of what?"

"Of . . . of *everything*."

"I don't understand."

"Oh, you know. The editorial. The protest. Murray and that crowd were dead set against it. Everybody at that party will be an *enemy*."

"Really, Summer, you are far too young to have enemies. And besides, that's all the more reason for you to go. You need to make friends with your classmates again. You need to make up with them. After all, they're the ones you'll be going through school with, not Rod Whitman."

Dad came in just then, and rifled through the drawers for matches.

"What's up?" he wondered.

"Summer has been invited to a New Year's Eve party at the Hamms'. I think she ought to go. Children her own age will be there."

"What's the problem?" Dad asked me.

I knew I could have won that argument in a second. All I'd have to do was tell them that Murray's parents weren't going to be home and that his purple-nailed sister was going to be entertaining older kids upstairs. How *far* upstairs I wouldn't even have to mention. But I'd sworn not to tell. And if I did tell and my parents told the Hamms, I'd never be able to show my face in school again. I'd have to leave town with a gypsy caravan. So I kept my mouth shut about all that.

"Dad, I don't like the kids who are going to be there, and they don't like me. It'll be awful."

"You don't know that unless you go," Mother said. "Besides, why would they invite you if they didn't like you?"

I couldn't answer that. It occurred to me that they might be planning to burn me at the stake. But from my parents' point of view, of course, it all seemed like an ordinary, civilized party, complete with chaperones.

"It sounds as if they're trying to make up with you, Summer," Dad suggested.

That did it. Dad was lined up on Mother's side. With the last glimmer of hope fading fast, I called Terry to see if he would be at the party. There was no answer.

The afternoon of the party, Mother seemed very chipper, laying out my dress and lending me a pair of pantyhose. I got the feeling she and I were on a seesaw: When I was up, she was down. Now she was up and I was way, way down.

I felt weird in a dress; it'd been ages since I'd seen my legs without slacks or jeans. I wore boots and carried my heels until Dad let me out at the Hamms' house. Murray, all decked out in a suit and bow tie (a bow tie!) opened the door. His metallic grin positively glittered. I waved to Dad.

"See you at twelve thirty," he called, backing out of the driveway.

It was eight thirty then. I had four hours to spend in hell.

"Couldn't you have gotten here without him?" Murray hissed.

125

"No, I couldn't."

"Well, he might have noticed that one of my parents' cars is gone."

"So? Your sister could have taken it."

"Mmmm, I guess. Well, come on in. Everybody's downstairs."

"Let me change my shoes," I said, grumpily. We were off to a great start.

I left my boots dripping in the hall and followed Murray through a horde of noisy older kids spread over the living room. Through the kitchen we trudged and down the basement steps. After the brightness upstairs, the recreation room seemed to be one shade brighter than pitch-black. About four candles glimmered here and there. At first, I could hardly see. Soon, I wished I couldn't see at all. Two couples were slow-dancing to a Barbra Streisand record. Another couple was wedged into an easy chair near the stairs. Cokes and bowls of pretzels and potato chips were lined up on the bar, surrounded by a knot of boys. A group of girls huddled on a sofa across the room.

Someone yelled, "Hi, Summer." I said hi toward the voice and somebody else giggled. Or should I say, "cackled"? It was old Witch Warren, herself. As my eyes adjusted to the dark, I realized there wasn't a soul there I cared to talk to, let alone spend four hours with.

Murray asked me to dance. I thought that was very nice of him and tried not to gag on the spicy cologne or after-shave lotion he was wearing. He must have *bathed* in it. I was arranging my head so my glasses wouldn't pierce his ear when he announced:

"My mother says I have to dance at least once with

every girl at a party. I think it's stupid, so I get it over with right away."

"Murray," I said, "if you don't like me, why did you invite me to this party?"

"My mother says if I give a party, I have to invite the whole class. I shouldn't play favorites."

"But your parents aren't here. They don't even know you're having this party."

Murray grinned his idiot grin. "I guess they're here in spirit," he said.

Part of their spirit landed on my lenses.

Suddenly there was a shriek from the easy chair, followed by yelps and whistles from the boys at the bar. We all looked over just in time to see Beverly Watkins remove Paul DuBerry's hand from her left breast. It was pretty obvious we'd been invited to see it. They looked around, laughing and pretending to be embarrassed, then they went back to kissing. There were several more hoots and hollars from that corner. It made me very nervous. In fact, I thought I was going to throw up.

In between leers at Beverly, Murray muttered that he'd ended up with seven girls and six boys because so many kids had gone away for the holidays.

"If I'd known Terry was out of town, I probably wouldn't have invited you," he admitted.

"Thanks," I said.

The song ended, about three minutes too late, as far as I was concerned.

"Tank you very mooch," Murray said, in a bad Count Dracula accent.

"You're velcum," I told him and wandered over to the

127

bar. The guys there mumbled "hi" shyly, as if we'd never met before. Then a fast dance started and everybody grabbed a partner. Except me. Three dances later, I was still munching pretzels and wishing I were dead. It wasn't that I wanted to dance with anybody there. Given the choice, I'd pay *not* to dance with them. But even Murray Hamm spitting on your glasses is better than being so obviously alone in a crowd.

For a while, I tried tapping my foot and singing along, as if I enjoyed watching other people dance. That quickly got to feeling phony, so I worked up a coughing spell and put a lot of energy and care into pouring myself a Coke. Before I could decide what to do with myself next, the record ended and somebody blew out all the candles. I felt a hand whisk across my chest. I gasped and a fake voice cackled, "Whoops, wrong boob." The next thing I knew, everybody was paired off, tucked into corners and making out like crazy.

Except me.

I groped for the stairs, stumbled up a few, and sat down. A huge lump burned in my throat. I won't cry, I told myself. Stupid and humiliating as this is, I will not give them the satisfaction of seeing me cry. Then, I thought, ha! Nobody would see me cry because nobody was paying me the least bit of attention. I was the Original Invisible Girl. Yelps and squeals and giggles shot up from the darkness like arrows aimed at my heart. I gulped down my lump and struggled the rest of the way up to the door.

There was one fluorescent light on over the kitchen sink. The rest of the first floor was dark. Apparently the

128

two parties weren't much different from each other after all.

I sat down at the kitchen table and tried to think what to do. The clock over the stove said nine thirty-six. There was a phone on the wall right next to me. I could call Dad, I supposed, but then, when I left, I'd have to fight my way through the darkened living room, past who knows what. I'd have to put my boots on in the dark, too, if I could even find them. I'd also have to explain why there were no lights on.

Tears rolled down my cheeks. It wasn't the humiliation so much by then. It was the irony of it all. Here I am, Mother, I wanted to scream. Partying with children my own age. Whoopee and Happy New Year. I stood up and yanked a tissue out of a box on the counter and blew my nose, loud and long. Suddenly, there were footsteps behind me. I spun around, tissue to nose, and came face to face with Rod Whitman! I blinked. He was still there. Quickly, I grabbed another tissue for my eyes and then crumpled them both together and threw them away.

"Summer! What are you doing here?" he was saying, as if he hadn't just caught me honking my nose off.

"Celebrating New Year's Eve," I answered, smiling weakly.

He laughed. "Yeah, me too." He sat down at the table and motioned me to sit opposite him.

"I didn't see you when I came in," I said.

"No, I got here late. Too late," he said, rolling his eyes suggestively.

"Everybody's paired off, huh?" I said, trying not to blush.

129

"Yup, and I do have to be faithful to Cindy."

And Reggie, I thought. And me, a little voice squeaked in the back of my brain. I told it to shut up.

"So, what's happening downstairs?" Rod asked.

I wished he hadn't. "Same thing as upstairs," I muttered. My bottom lip started to quiver. I bit it, hard.

"Nobody you're interested in?" That was a nice way to put it, I thought.

"It's not my gang," I said. "My mother made me come."

Rod nodded. "Yeah, I know the scene."

I couldn't even look at him. I was so embarrassed. Suddenly, he jumped to his feet. Oh, God, I thought, don't leave me here alone. I'll die!

But he only went to the refrigerator. "Want a Coke?" he called over his shoulder.

"Okay," I said, even though the one I'd just finished was still gurgling.

He glanced at the clock. "Two hours and fifteen minutes to the New Year," he said. "I'm here because of my parents, too. They don't like to see me mope. I'm supposed to have a good time for the three of us."

There was a transistor radio on the counter. Rod turned it on. The rock station was having a nostalgia night to send off the old year. Some ancient Johnny Mathis record was playing.

"So, let's have a good time," Rod said. "Shall we dance?"

My mouth fell open. Slow-dancing with Murray was one thing. Who cared if I broke all his toes? But with Rod! I looked at my hands. They were damp from the Coke

130

bottle. As I wiped them quickly on a napkin, the world's smallest voice piped up and said, "Okay." Was that me?

The next thing I knew, I was in Rod's arms, dancing. Even with my heels on, I didn't come up to his shoulders. I put my cheek against his sweater. It was soft and tickly. But my glasses got in the way, so I had to realign my head. Rod didn't smell spicy like Murray. He smelled clean. His hand, pressing ever so gently on my back, was burning a hole right through to my stomach. I don't think I breathed the whole time we were dancing, I was concentrating so hard on following. I only tipped his foot once. A surface injury, nothing major. Actually, he was such a good dancer, a five-legged elephant could have followed him. When the song ended, and a hamburger ad came on, he looked down at me and smiled. "That was fun," he said.

I nodded. Where were all the conversational questions I'd thought up for the day he used Dad's files? Gone. I was speechless.

"Maybe my parents were right," Rod said as we went back to our Cokes. "Maybe this will be a nice evening after all."

He was going to stay with me! That's what he was saying. I glanced at the clock. Just over two hours until midnight. That wasn't long enough! I wanted it to be more! And to think, only an hour earlier I had been wishing the time away.

Every time the disc jockey played a record, we danced. And through the ads and chatter and weather and news, we talked. Both the dancing and the talking got easier and easier to do.

"My parents are pretty old," Rod admitted. "They got

131

married when Mom was thirty-five and Dad was forty. Mom was thirty-eight when she had me."

"That was pretty brave," I said, "having a baby when you're that old."

"Yeah. I could have been deformed or something."

And you could have been an abortion, I heard Reggie's voice say.

"My parents were older, too," I said, "but not as old as yours. I think I was a mistake, actually."

"No, you weren't."

"I mean it," I said. Then I told him about the scrapbooks and how Mother sometimes looked at me as if I were a visitor from outer space.

"Oh, you must be imagining that." Rod laughed. For some reason, he never seemed to see the truth about me, how really insignificant I was.

"Do your parents expect Douglas to make them happy all the time?" he asked suddenly.

"What do you mean?"

"I mean, does he have to be successful all the time? Do all the right things? Go to all the right places?"

"Well, I don't know. Douglas always *is* successful, but I don't know if it's for them or just because that's the way he is."

"Hmmmm," Rod said, frowning.

"Why do you ask?"

"Oh, I don't know." He shrugged, rolling his Coke bottle between his hands.

"Do you have to be successful for your parents?" I asked.

He looked at me for a minute and then said, "Yeah, I do. They make me feel like . . . like they can't be happy unless I'm happy. But I have to be a certain *kind* of happy. I have to play basketball. My dad could have had a basketball scholarship to college, but he had to work to support his family. I have to be popular. You know, be with the right crowd. Stuff like that."

We were quiet for a while. It was hard for me to imagine someone being popular because they *had* to. Most kids would give anything to be as popular as Rod. Then Rod spoke up again, not looking at me.

"That's why I wasn't in the senior play. I'm no actor."

"Well, very few of them were. They just had fun."

"But I can't . . . I can't . . ."

"You can't have fun?"

"No, I mean, I can't *just* have fun. Get out there in front of everybody and make a spectacle of myself."

"But you get out there every time you play basketball."

"That's different. I'm good at basketball."

"Oh. You mean you can't fail."

Something very much like gratitude glowed in Rod's eyes. "Yes," he said. "Yes, that's it. That's exactly it. I *have* to succeed. All the time. Or I feel like I'm letting them down. God, I've never talked to anybody about this before."

Not even Cindy? I wondered. But I preferred not to bring her up just then.

"Let's dance," Rod said, suddenly. It was another slow one. He held me much tighter than before, so tight I couldn't breathe if I wanted to. But I didn't want to.

133

We were chatting away like old buddies when Murray's sister and some guy I didn't know wandered in. They looked at us, bleary-eyed. The guy held out a crumpled cigarette to Rod. Rod shook his head. I knew from the sweet smell that it was pot. It made me very nervous just to be in the same room with it. I expected police to crash through the window and cart us all away. I was really glad Rod didn't smoke any.

Murray's sister opened the refrigerator like a sleepwalker and stared into it for a long time. Then she started to giggle. The guy went over and stared with her and giggled, too. Murray's sister began to lift out bottles of Coke, one after the other.

"One for you and one for you and one for you," she kept saying, handing the guy more and more Cokes. They were both laughing their heads off. Rod and I looked at each other. We started to laugh, too, but I was still kind of scared. I wished they'd go away.

"One for you and one for you and one for you . . ."

Any second now, the guy was going to drop those Cokes. We'd be stuck cleaning up the mess, probably. Rod must have been thinking the same thing because he got up and took the Cokes away from him.

"Okay, kiddies," he said. "One to a customer. One for you and one for you, and bye-bye."

"Yes, sir, Dad," the guy said. He and Murray's sister thought that was hilarious. Leaning on each other for support, they staggered, howling, back to the living room. Rod grinned at me and shrugged his shoulders.

"Did you ever try it?" I asked him.

"Yeah."

"What's it like?"

"Well, it doesn't make me act stupid, like that," he said. "Maybe I'm too uptight. Mainly, it makes me hungry as hell."

"Sounds dumb."

"Yeah. I think it is."

Suddenly, there was screaming and horns blowing all over the house. We looked at the clock. It was midnight!

"Hey." Rod grinned, taking my face in his hands. "Happy New Year, kid."

And he kissed me. Right on the lips. It was like a lightning bolt shooting straight through me. My first kiss, I thought, and I'll never be able to tell Reggie about it!

The basement door burst open just then. The crowd from below exploded into the kitchen, horns blaring. Marjory Warren was one of the first. She looked from Rod to me and then back again. And I knew I'd better tell Reggie before someone else did.

# 16

I began a letter to Reggie. Seven times. Then I realized she probably wouldn't get the letter in time anyway. She was due home Wednesday the fourth. I'd just have to be the first person on the phone to her house that day.

I spent as much time as possible shoveling snow. I needed new clothes, particularly something terrific to wear to the basketball game Tuesday night. I had some money my grandparents had sent me for Christmas, but I wanted enough for a whole new outfit, head to toe.

Besides, getting out meant I didn't have to talk to my parents much. I told them I had a very nice time at the party. That made them very pleased with themselves. They each said, "See? You never know unless you try," two or three times, and I tried my best to look as if I'd learned a truly valuable lesson that I would carry with me into adulthood.

Or, at least, out into the snow. And whom did I spy shoveling away right down the block but Rod Whitman!

"Hi, kiddo," he called. "Am I on your territory?"

I loved the way he called me kiddo. It made being a kid worthwhile.

"No, I'm looking for new territory. I've been all the way around the block. Hey, doesn't shoveling snow make your arms too stiff for basketball? I can hardly move mine at the end of a day."

"Well, I won't do it tomorrow. But no, not usually. It's really pretty good exercise. Tell you what. Let's shovel together and split the money."

"That's not fair. You'll do more of the work than I will."

"How do you know? Maybe I'm very lazy." He grinned. Lazy or not, he sure was handsome. Even with a bright-red nose.

So, side by side, we shoveled. He did do more than me—than I—but he never complained about it. We laughed a lot. But we worked hard. In fact, I practically broke my back trying to do a fair share. By late afternoon, we had fifteen dollars each.

"What are you going to spend your loot on?" Rod asked.

"Oh, clothes and stuff," I said. "How about you?"

"Tickets to the Sweetheart Dance. It's lucky we've had all this snow. Valentine's Day comes too close to Christmas for me."

The Sweetheart Dance! Had I helped him shovel snow so he could take Cindy Grant to the Sweetheart Dance? Part of me thought that stank, and part of me thought, well, what are friends for? And another part of me, the really sneaky part, was thinking that Valentine's Day was over a month away and a lot could happen in that time. Look at what had happened in these few days!

"Want some hot chocolate?" I offered when we were both finally too cold and tired to go on.

"Sure would," he said. We trudged back to my house. He carried both shovels. When we arrived, Dad was backing out of the driveway. He rolled down his window.

"Your mother's out," he announced.

"Okay," I replied. "We're going to have some hot chocolate."

Dad looked doubtful. "Oh, well," he said, hesitantly, "I need to run over to my office for a few minutes. I'll be right back."

"Don't rush," I said, with a big, teasing smile. I knew he wasn't worried about me being alone with Rod. He was worried about *Mother* being worried about it. He pulled his eyebrows together above his nose. I giggled and led Rod around to the back of the house. We stashed the shovels in the garage and then attacked our boots on the back porch.

It's not easy to look graceful while tugging at slick, wet,

138

tight boots with frozen hands. Rod, of course, slipped out of his with the greatest of ease. I hopped around and puffed and huffed and practically bowled myself over.

"Have a seat," Rod suggested, indicating the floor. I sat. He grabbed my right foot and started pulling. Instead of the boot coming off, I went sliding across the porch on my rear.

"Stop! I'll get splinters!" I screamed.

Laughing, Rod spun me around by the boot and started bouncing me up and down. The boot loosened and then shot off. He went crashing over Mother's cardboard boxes full of gardening equipment and slammed into the storm door. We laughed until tears ran down our faces. Every time he tried to pull off my other boot, we started howling again. Finally, with me braced in the doorway, he ripped off the other boot and we staggered into the kitchen, weak from laughing so hard.

Over the hot chocolate, we got very quiet.

"Oh, this is nice and peaceful." I sighed. "It hasn't been this way around here for a long time."

"What do you mean?"

"Oh, I don't know. My mother and I are having some kind of war. I'm not even sure what about. But it's been going on ever since I wrote that editorial and became Public Enemy Number One."

"Oh, come on. You're a *hero*. I mean, a heroine."

"Oh, yeah, sure." I sighed again. "Not to my mother. Lately, she's been crying over *everything*. The only time she seems happy is when she's making me unhappy."

"Like sending you to Murray's party."

139

"Exactly."

"Maybe she's got what my parents have: Be-happy-through-your-children-itis."

"No. If she did, she'd *want* me to be a heroine, wouldn't she?"

"Well, a certain kind of heroine. Not just any old kind."

"You mean a swimming and diving champ, like she was?"

"That's the way it works in my family."

I shook my head and took a sip of hot chocolate. "No. That's not it. Not for me and Mother, anyway. She never even taught me how to swim. I went off and did it myself. I always go off and do things myself. She never pushes me to do anything at all."

Suddenly, something became very clear to me. "What she wants," I said, very slowly, "what she's always wanted, is for me to stay out of her way. Not bother her. And until that editorial thing, that's exactly what I've always done."

"Weird," Rod said. "My parents push me to be a star, and yours push you to be a nothing."

"A nothing," I echoed. An abortion, I thought. I shouldn't have been born. But having been born, I was supposed to go on acting as if I hadn't. The Original Invisible Girl. Do Not Notice.

"Well, it's been okay up till now," I said, talking as much to myself as to Rod. "Mother was never thrilled with me, but she was never angry with me either. Now she's angry with me all the time. I bother her no matter what I do. And you know what? I'm glad!"

"You are?"

I nodded. "I don't really mean I'm glad to bother her. What I'm glad about is *being somebody*, for a change. I never thought I'd like it, but I do. God, I hated all that attention. But now, I'm kind of proud of the whole thing."

"Well, you should be."

"And to think I was so scared I thought I'd die!"

"I'll never believe that. You looked like you knew exactly what you were doing."

"That's amazing. You know, though, if I had to do it all over again, I think I really would know what I was doing. Of course, it might be even harder, knowing what it would do to Mother. It's funny. Kids used to envy me for having a famous mother. If they only knew . . ."

"What's the big deal, anyway, between your mother and an eighth-grade editorial? I don't get it."

"Oh, it's not so much the article itself—although she was against it. It was the wire-service report on it. That got some weirdo reporter interested in an article on Mother, a "Whatever Happened to America's Mermaid" kind of thing. Mother got all upset and refused to give him an interview. So he sold a picture of her to *National Gossip*, with a caption saying she was hiding middle-age flab."

"*Your* mother? *Middle-age flab*? I know girls in high school who would pay good money to have a body like hers. Hell, they *do* pay good money—for dancing lessons and clothes and diet pills. They talk about her all the time. They think she's beautiful. And she is. But I guess you know that."

141

I sighed. "Yes, I know."

There was an extremely awkward silence. I knew Rod was thinking he ought to say I was good-looking, too, but in all honesty, he couldn't. He looked so uncomfortable, I had to laugh.

"It's all right," I said. "I know I'm plain. Douglas got her looks. I got Daddy's eyesight."

Rod saw the polite way out and grabbed it. "You're not plain," he said.

"Well, I'm certainly not fancy. Anyway, that *National Gossip* thing really set Mother off. I feel terrible about it, but what can I do?"

"Nothing. I mean, I still don't understand why she's upset. It's not as if she really *were* hiding middle-age flab."

"That's what Dad and I keep telling her. But she just starts crying all over again. I think she's okay when she's at the gym, working. I guess keeping busy helps. But the minute she walks in the door here, she gets a headache and goes upstairs and lies down. Or she screams at me for nothing at all, like leaving one dirty cup in the sink. Or she just stares into the distance, with this hopeless look on her face. Do you think she's going crazy?"

"No," Rod said, drawing the *o* out slowly, as a thought dawned on his face. "I think she's going through menopause."

"*What?*" I had my hot-chocolate cup raised to my lips just then and almost poured it all down the front of my sweater.

"Menopause. My mother went through it when I was

142

around ten. She cried a lot, too. My father explained it to me. It's when a woman stops menstruating and sometimes her hormone balance gets out of whack for a while and she gets very moody."

"I know," I squeaked, burying a blush behind my cup. I couldn't believe he'd just come out and said that. I'd never discussed stuff like that with a boy, not even Terry. In fact, I'd never even discussed it with my parents. They left books in my room for me to read, as needed. Or as they thought they were needed. Actually, Reggie was always one book ahead of me and kept me posted.

"She'll be okay after a while," Rod went on. "But you're right, keeping busy helps. My mother went back to work, and it made all the difference in the world."

"But my mother already works," I said.

"Then I guess you'll just have to sweat it out."

Dad came roaring up the driveway then. From the way he zoomed through the door, I think he was expecting to find me in bed with Rod. He looked surprised and relieved to find us innocently sipping hot chocolate. (And discussing Mother's menopause!)

Rod polished off his last sip and stood up. "Guess I'll be on my way," he said. "Thanks for the hot chocolate."

"You're welcome," I said. We both laughed when he started to put on his boots.

"On is easier than off."

"It would have to be," I agreed.

"Well, 'bye, kid, see you tomorrow."

"Oh. Rod?"

"Yes?"

"Thanks."

"For what?"

"Oh, you know. Listening and stuff."

"Anytime, kiddo."

Dreamily, I turned from the door. And met dad's questioning glance. Questioning? *Accusing*.

"Oh, Dad!" I wailed. "Really, you're getting as bad as Mother."

I tried to zip past him and get to my room, but he caught me by the elbow.

"What do you mean by that?" he asked, not angry, but pretty firm.

"I mean, you're acting as if I were—as if I were having an *affair*, or something. You look so *suspicious*—"

"Concerned."

"Well, for Pete's sake, can't two people have a friendship in peace?"

"I don't know, Summer," he said, quietly. "Can they?"

I couldn't answer. I couldn't even look him in the eye. Because I honestly didn't know.

# 17

I got this really fantastic blue pantsuit to wear to the basketball game. It was the same blue as the sweater Rod wore New Year's Eve. I spotted it from halfway across the store. I swear elves must have spent hours stitching it up especially for me, because it fit like nothing else I've ever owned. It even looked okay with my boots, which my parents insisted I wear instead of the neat Casual Walking Shoes I bought with my last $10.95 plus tax. They insisted I return those because I really didn't need them. Well, I was brand new and stunning from head to ankle, anyway.

After soaking forty-five minutes in the tub with Mother's bath oil, I shampooed my hair three times. I used a round brush to turn under the ends while I blew it dry. I knew it would go straight again the minute I walked outside, but I had to try. A little lipstick, both of my charm bracelets, four rings and a pendant necklace later, I felt ready. Then I looked at myself in the full-length mirror on Mother's closet door. I looked as if I were suited up for an elegant ladies' luncheon instead of a basketball game. I stripped off the jewelry, except for the rings. That helped. Then I took off two rings and that helped even more.

"Maybe I'll stay and watch the game," Dad said as he pulled up in front of the gym.

"Dad! You've got to be kidding!" I yelped.

"Yes, I've got to be kidding," he assured me and leaned my way for a kiss.

"I can't. My lipstick," I said.

So he brushed a kiss across my forehead. It was odd for him to kiss me anyway, I thought, until I noticed the expression on his face. It was full of that "my-little-girl-is-growing-up" look you see on TV commercials. Usually, the next line is "Do you have enough life insurance?" But in our case, it was "Remember, you come back to the house after the game."

"Okay," I said, "but you and Mother better not be sitting there like the guards at Buckingham Palace."

"The guards at Buckingham Palace stand."

"*Dad!*"

"Don't worry, we won't embarrass you."

One more good-bye and I jumped out of the car to slosh

146

along with the crowd toward the entrance. The gym really looked different. Of course, I'd never seen it at night. The crowd and the band playing and all that stuff made it pretty exciting. It was hard to believe the last time I'd been there was at the Christmas program. That seemed to have happened a hundred years ago.

At first, I didn't see anyone I knew, which was just as well. University School was playing Roxbury, the other high school in town, so the crowd was equally divided. I grabbed the first empty seat I came to, right near the door. I didn't even think about sitting in the right section—until the Roxbury cheerleaders lined up right in front of me and started rooting for their team. By then, it was too late to move. The bleachers were packed.

The P.A. system screeched itself to life and somebody whose voice I didn't recognize started announcing the players. I thought I was the only one who stayed seated as the Roxbury team trotted out. I couldn't decide whether or not to stand up for our team. I didn't want to be all alone up there. Three or four other people near me stood up, though, so I did, too. It was kind of embarrassing, but at least I wasn't the only displaced person.

I thought I saw Rod glance toward the bleachers as if he were searching for someone. If it was me, he certainly didn't find me.

After a while, even though I don't care for sports, I got pretty worked up. The score seesawed back and forth, and a knot tightened in my stomach every time Roxbury surged ahead. At the half, we were trailing by six. Three times—practically all by himself—Rod closed the gap for

University. But Roxbury finally won, 67–65. The Roxbury fans around me ran out onto the court and screamed and threw hats and all kinds of junk into the air. The University people just shuffled out quickly, muttering with their heads bowed. A lot of people take the competition between University and Roxbury very seriously.

I lost track of Rod. He'd told me to wait for him in the gym, so I moved over to what had been the University cheering section. Someone had left a program behind. I busied myself studying it. All of a sudden, I got that queer feeling that comes over you when you're being watched. Prickles on the back of the neck. I looked up from the program. The gym was almost empty. But there, at the far door, was none other than Marjory Warren. The minute I spotted her, she disappeared. No doubt she was wondering why I was hanging around after the game. Or, more likely, she'd guessed why.

Ten, fifteen, twenty minutes crawled by. The crowd was gone; only a few people were left here and there. A couple made their way down the bleachers and sat in the first row, staring straight ahead. They were older, maybe in their late fifties, I thought. The man was tall and held himself very erect. Suddenly, it dawned on me that they were Rod's parents. Should I say hello? Well, I'd never been introduced, so I guessed not. Besides, they looked so unhappy, I wouldn't know what to say.

It seemed forever until Rod finally came out of the locker room. But it had been worth the wait. Except that he wasn't smiling, he looked terrific, all fresh-scrubbed and squeaky-clean. I stood up and he sent me a sorrowful wave. Then he went over to his parents. Once again, I didn't know what to do. Should I join them? There I stood, hesitating and feeling terrifically foolish. Finally, Mr. and Mrs. Whitman left and Rod came toward me.

"Hi," he said, not very cheerfully.

"Hi," I said. "I'm sorry you lost."

He nodded and shrugged. "Well, where would you like to go?"

"Oh . . . um . . . home."

He looked surprised, which was certainly understandable.

"We have a houseful of food and my parents suggested we . . . ah . . . enjoy it."

"Are you sure?"

I nodded.

"As pretty as you look, I really ought to take you somewhere and show you off."

As usual, I blushed. And blew the compliment.

"Oh, this is just something I—found." Spent three hours searching for! And two more hours arranging on my body!

"Well, shall we?" Rod offered.

I followed him outside. It was lucky I'd worn my boots because we walked home. In my Casual Walking Shoes, I'd have had frostbitten toes, not to mention soggy Casual Walking Shoes.

"I'd really like a cup of the usual," Rod said, as soon as we got in the back door. I'd purposely worn only stockings under my boots so I could slip them off without the floor-bouncing routine.

The house was unusually silent.

"Mother? Dad? We're home," I called up the stairs. A faint "okay" wafted back at me. Well, at least they were upholding their half of the promise and staying out of sight.

There's something about being dressed up that makes me very shy. I was glad I had to bustle around boiling water for the hot chocolate and opening peanuts and pretzels. Rod slumped into a kitchen chair and held his head between his hands, his elbows propped on his knees.

"Are you okay?" I asked.

"Oh, sure. Tired. Disappointed. Worried. But okay."

"I can understand tired and disappointed. But why worried?"

Rod straightened up, then leaned his head back against the wall. "I've been offered a basketball scholarship to University."

"That's terrific," I said, but his reaction wasn't what I expected. He didn't even smile. "Isn't it?" I added, uncertainly.

"Well, it's an honor. But it means I'd have to stay here. College would be like four more years of high school."

The kettle started to whistle. I snatched it off the burner before it rose to a full shriek. Rod ignored it and kept talking.

"I was hoping to go away to college. And not play basketball."

150

"Really? Don't you like to play basketball? You look like you're enjoying it." I set the refreshments out on the table. "Hey, would you like to move into the living room? We don't have to stay in the kitchen."

"I kind of like it here. This will be our third kitchen date of the year. It's a tradition."

"Okay," I smiled. Kitchens would never again be the same for me.

"I really do enjoy basketball. I couldn't have done as well if I didn't. But I've kind of had enough, you know? I don't want to be a pro."

"But your parents want you to?"

"I don't know if they think that far ahead. Probably. What they want now is for me to play for University. Dad's a good friend of Coach Jeffries and all that. And, of course, Cindy's going to University."

"She is?" I gulped, as nonchalantly as possible.

"Oh, yes. There's been a member of her family at University since the school was founded."

"Another tradition," I said, weakly.

We were quiet for a minute, sipping and staring into the distance. Finally, I said, "What do *you* want to do, Rod?"

"That's the worst of it. I don't know. It's been so comfortable here, playing ball, being a school hero, dating Cindy. It's all been planned for me for so long, I've never thought out any plans for myself."

"It was planned for you to date Cindy?"

"Well, maybe not planned, but definitely encouraged. Our folks have been friends since the dawn of civilization.

I think they had us paired off in the hospital nursery."

"I thought—I thought you really *liked* Cindy."

"Well, I did. I still do. Except our relationship has changed. A lot."

I waited. Rod fiddled with some peanuts.

"And it bothers me. A lot," he went on. Then he stalled again. I took a pretzel and broke it, munched one end, and waited.

"I've never talked to anybody about this," he said. "You've got to swear never to tell *anyone*."

I wasn't sure I wanted to hear what Rod was about to say, but he didn't even wait for me to swear.

"Cindy has this cousin in Chicago," he said, more to the peanuts than to me. "The one she's visiting now, Susannah. And this Susannah—who's a year older than Cindy—talked Cindy into going on the Pill."

I started choking on pretzel salt. Rod had to slam me on the back to stop my coughing. "Sorry, pretzel salt," I wheezed.

He got me a glass of water, which I gulped down too quickly and started coughing again. You'd think my near death by strangulation would knock him off the track, but it didn't.

"Where was I?" he said. I didn't tell him. But he remembered. "Oh, yes, Cindy's cousin and the Pill. Yeah, well, Susannah set up the appointment with the doctor and everything. It sounded like some kind of weird joke to me, but Cindy took it very seriously. *Very* seriously. When she came home from Chicago last summer, we started—making it."

Was I dizzy from choking or was I simply about to faint? Either way, unconscious sounded like a good state to be in.

"And ever since then, we don't talk anymore. We just—make it. Not that I don't enjoy it, but . . . we don't talk anymore."

Now he focused his eyes on me. I tried desperately to look calm and mature.

"Like you and I are talking right now. It's important to me. There are people who would laugh their heads off if I said this, but it's more important to me than (Oh, God, I thought, don't say it. I really can't handle this.) sex. Does that make any sense to you?"

"Oh, sure," I said. My own sex life being what it was, I would certainly have to agree that talking was more important.

"It's all been too easy for me, Summer. I know that sounds like a ridiculous complaint. I guess I'm a real ingrate. But everything's been set up for me for so long, I don't know if I could go out and try something on my own. All I know is, I'd like to, but the thought scares the hell out of me."

He looked at me with a pained expression, like a puppy who needed to be taken in out of the rain.

"Well," I said, "I went through something that scared the hell out of me. But it didn't kill me."

"Oh, you weren't that scared," he insisted. Why couldn't he believe that? "Besides, you're stronger than I am."

"What? You've got to be kidding."

"No, I mean it. There's a *strength* about you. I can feel it. That's one of the things I really like about you. When I'm with you, I feel stronger."

"Rod, I've never done a strong thing in my entire life. Oh, so I wrote an editorial and got sucked into a protest demonstration. Big deal."

"It *is* a big deal. You are a strong person, Summer."

"I am?"

Rod was about to answer when we heard a highly artificial cough, followed by footsteps on the stairs.

"Summer, it's after midnight," Dad said, obviously embarrassed to be saying it. Mother must have sent him down to deliver the message. "I heard about the game on the news, Rod," he went on. "Sorry about the loss."

"Well, thanks," Rod said. He stood up and put on his jacket. "Win or lose, I'm pretty tired. Thanks again for the food, Summer."

"Anytime," I said, trying to sound light and cheerful, as if we'd spent the last hour discussing peanuts.

Dad lingered in the kitchen while Rod got his boots on. Did he think Rod was going to kiss me good night? I hadn't thought about it myself, and wouldn't have, except for Dad's standing there like that, ill at ease but very much present and at attention.

"Good night," Rod said. "See you in school Thursday. Good night, Dr. Smith."

"Okay," I said, closing the door and locking it behind him. When I turned around, Dad had disappeared, his duty done. Parents! *Honestly!*

154

I called Reggie's house about every half hour all day Wednesday. No one answered. I didn't see her until I arrived at school Thursday morning. I didn't have to look twice to know that Marjory Warren had gotten to her first.

# 18

Do you have any idea what it's like to go to school every day when half the kids think you're weird and the other half hate you outright and your best friend refuses to speak to you? It's not good for your complexion, let me tell you. In two weeks' time, my chin looked like the Alps in miniature, and not even a half gallon of Pretty Foxy Medicated Natural Cover-Up could help.

That first day back to school, I greeted Reggie with all the true joy I felt on seeing her again—and, I thought, not a trace of the guilt I also felt. All to no avail. She would not speak to me. In fact, she made a special point of sticking close to Marjory and her stuck-up, snobby bunch.

I cornered her once in the girls' locker room and told her I could explain everything if she'd give me a chance, but she refused. Well, I wasn't going to beg, so I gave up.

To make matters worse, somebody had ratted on Murray Hamm and his sister and they were both grounded for two months. Of course, Murray thought it was me. The more I insisted it wasn't, the less he believed me. So I gave up on that, too. Much later, one of Murray's sister's friends confessed, but that didn't save me from several weeks of pure torture.

The only person who stuck by me was Terry. Of course, to him I was another hopeless cause that he couldn't resist taking on. Well, maybe that's unfair. He's a loyal friend, and I was grateful to have his company there on death row.

Perfect strangers glared at me when I walked down the halls. I didn't know if they were Marjory's friends or Cindy's friends or Murray's sister's friends, or what. For all I knew, they were blaming me for radioactive fallout and all the starving children in Asia.

The class tittered at every move I made. I got absolutely paralyzed after a while. Poor Mrs. Morton kept trying to rekindle that spark she'd seen when I wrote the editorial. She asked my opinion about everything and suggested extra work I might be interested in doing. She looked terribly disappointed when I had no opinions to offer on any subject whatsoever and politely declined the extra work, no matter how fascinating. It was all I could do to keep up with the regular work. When you're lonely and depressed, merely getting your name down on paper takes tremendous effort. I hated to hurt Mrs. Morton's feelings, but what could I do? There's no explaining to a teacher what *really* goes on in a classroom.

And what was Rod Whitman doing all this time, you might well ask? Well, he wasn't holding Cindy's hand, but he wasn't holding mine, either. The most I got was a sickly smile whenever we passed in the hall—and he always passed quickly, before I could say anything. He could usually be found trailing Cindy with an apologetic look on his face that showed signs of becoming permanent. She, on the other hand, would go bustling on ahead, ignoring him. Her girl friends surrounded her, bearing their textbooks and purses like shields.

What really hurt was his acting as if we'd actually done something wrong. I'd been a friend to him. I'd listened to his confessions and I hadn't told anyone. If I could have told Reggie, it might have changed her attitude toward me. But I wasn't going to tell her, even though I hadn't sworn, technically. It seemed to me that if Rod could have been open about our friendship, if he'd dared to walk right over and talk to me, it would have changed a lot of attitudes. When the big man on campus approves of somebody, it's very hard for the little people to disapprove. But he didn't. And that cut deeper than all the stares and titters and silences. Caring about one person can take a lot more out of you than caring about what a crowd thinks of you.

About two weeks into the semester, Terry and I were

standing at my locker after school, discussing a history quiz looming ahead, when Rod came down the otherwise deserted hall.

"Uh, Summer, could I talk to you for a minute?" he asked.

"Sure," I told him, trying to be very blasé and sophistocated about it.

"In private?" Rod went on. Terry gave him a mock bow and sauntered off with a jaunty "toodle-oo."

I looked up at Rod with what I hoped was an interested but not overwhelmed expression on my face. It didn't matter. He wasn't looking at me anyway.

"Um, Summer, there've been a lot of rumors about us lately. I guess you know that."

"Hmmmm," I said.

"And they've gotten to Cindy. I mean, I didn't help much. I told her I liked you a lot, which I do, but she took it wrong. She took it very seriously."

"Cindy always does," I muttered.

"There's nothing like that between us, is there?"

Now he looked at me. I stared him straight in the eye and said nothing. If the sky was going to fall, he was going to have to push it all by himself. How should I know what was between us? He had me very confused, to say the least. He was my first date and my first kiss. That was very important to me. But what was I to him? I was a thirteen-year-old kid and he was a seventeen-year-old who was "making it," as he so delicately put it. Let *him* figure it out.

"Is there?" he asked again, his voice cracking like a

twelve-year-old's. When I still didn't answer, he looked away again. "I didn't think so," he went on. It flashed across my mind that I could have changed the course of history if I'd said Yes, but it was too late. Anyway, he sounded relieved, as if my silence had let him off the hook. The rest of what he had to say sounded like a speech he'd rehearsed many times. In front of a mirror? In front of Cindy?

"Well, even though I value your friendship, I can't let it hurt Cindy, so I think it would be best for all concerned if you and I really cooled it." Oh, I thought, have we been heating it up? "Tonight, I'm going over to Cindy's house and I'm officially inviting her to the Sweetheart Dance. And I think if you and I kind of ignore each other, the whole problem will blow over pretty soon. At least, I hope so."

"Whatever you say, Rod," I said, totally amazed at my own cool.

"Thanks, Summer, you're a good kid."

"Sure am," I agreed. He started to walk away and then turned back.

"I accepted the scholarship," he said, avoiding my eyes.

"Congratulations," I said, trying hard to smile. But inside, I felt sorry for him. There's your big man on campus, I said to myself. Big star basketball player. And first-class coward. The minute he was out of sight, the floodgates broke. I leaned against my locker and bawled. I'd known he wasn't going to take me to the Sweetheart Dance. Any fool would have known that. But I guess way down deep, in that little secretly hopeful place, I'd thought maybe, *maybe* he would. And that wasn't the worst of it, anyway. The worst was knowing I'd been a friend to him and that he could shrug it off so easily. The approval of a clique of snobs was more important. It made me feel so small, so insignificant, so rotten.

I walked home under my own personal gray cloud, and it hovered over me all day. When I went to bed that night, there it was, like a canopy of gloom. In a miserable state, I dozed off. Then, suddenly, I was wide awake. The canopy cloud had vanished. And in its place was something as clear as the freshest, cleanest spring breeze in the world. *I was okay.* I'd felt small and insignificant lots of times, but it hadn't killed me. And I'd been the center of attention, too, good and bad, and that hadn't killed me either. I was Summer Smith and I knew it and I was glad. *That* was the strength Rod had talked about. I could feel it now, although it must have been there always.

And poor Rod, who had always been the center of attention, who had never been insignificant, he was the one who ran scared all the time. I'd tried to tell him that it was okay to be scared, that I'd been scared and survived—and even felt good about it afterward. But he hadn't believed me; he hadn't really listened.

Maybe someday he'll remember, though, and understand. I hope so.

# 19

Not one, but *two* girls on Mother's teams were going to try out for the Olympics. You'd have thought Mother would be ecstatic. You especially would have thought it from looking at the newspaper photos she posed for with them. The old America's Mermaid smile was in full blossom. Our phone rang day and night. Mother chattered like a schoolgirl to people she'd never said hello to before. But when the cameras were gone and the phone was quiet, the other side of her personality took over. Honestly, she was a female Dr. Jekyll and Mr. Hyde.

It was at its worst whenever she and I were alone

together. One night, about a week after Rod's sign-off, Dad was at a meeting of some kind and Mother and I were tackling a very odd vegetable soup.

"When are you going to return those shoes you bought?" she asked, out of nowhere.

"I decided not to. I can use them all spring and summer. Fall, too."

"With your jeans?"

"Well, I don't always wear jeans."

"You don't? Well, I guess not. Sometimes you wear pajamas."

I put down my soup spoon and drew myself up to my full seated height. "I do have articles of clothing other than jeans," I announced.

"Articles of clothing other than jeans. Well, la-di-da," she sang, bobbing her head side to side in a very irritating way.

"Don't make fun of me," I said.

"Don't you shout at me," she said.

"I wasn't shouting," I said. Loudly.

"You were, too," she insisted. Even louder.

"Well, if you didn't make fun of me, I wouldn't have to shout," I shouted.

"I was not making fun of you," she said. "I was merely telling you to return those shoes before it's too late and the store refuses to take them back."

"I don't want to return the shoes, and you can't make me do it because I spent my own hard-earned money on them. So there!"

"Don't you so-there me, young lady. I can make you do

whatever I need to make you do if you don't have the good sense to do it yourself. Now, you do not need those shoes. They are a waste of money, whoever's money it is. They don't go with your outfits, which are mainly jeans, and besides that, they make you look like a little old lady."

"Aha," I said. "Aha! That's it. They don't make me look like a little old lady at all. They make me look grown up. Well, I want to look grown up. Because I am grown up."

"Summer, you are thirteen years old."

"Nearly fourteen."

"Five months to go. Is it because of that boy? That what's-his-name Whitman? Is that why you want to look grown up?"

"No, it is not because of that what's-his-name Whitman. I want to look grown up because I *am* grown up. Or, at least, growing up."

She hadn't even listened. "Because let me tell you, if it is because of him, I am going to lay the law down right now: You are not to see him again. Is that clear? He is too old for you, no matter how grown up you imagine yourself to be. And that is that."

I nearly laughed in her face. But I sure didn't tell her what had already gone on between Rod and me. I wouldn't give her the satisfaction. I just gritted my teeth and stared her in the eye and let her think she was breaking up the hottest love affair since David and Bathsheba. I did have my pride, after all.

"Have I made myself understood?" she demanded, staring right back at me.

164

"Yes," I muttered.

"All right. Now finish your soup."

"It's cold."

"Heat it up."

"I don't want to," I mumbled. "It's awful."

"What?"

"I said it's awful. I don't know what you put into it this time, but it was a terrible mistake."

"What do you mean by 'this time'? You've never complained about my cooking before."

"I never complained about anything before," I said, mumbling again.

"Will you please stop that mumbling and speak so I can hear you?"

"I said I never complained about anything before."

"Now, *that* I can agree with," Mother said, whisking both soup bowls off the table and into the sink. She stayed at the sink with her back toward me. Somehow she looked kind of pathetic that way. "I really don't know what's gotten into you, Summer, but you are very hard to live with lately."

So are you, I thought. But I knew better than to say it, even as a mumble.

"I suppose this is what they mean by a stormy adolescence. Your brother never had one. He just got older and nicer each year."

I sighed. From remarks like that, I could easily learn to hate Douglas. Even if he really gets older and nicer every year, that didn't excuse her throwing him up to me like that.

165

I stood up and slapped my napkin down on the table. "Well, I'm not Douglas," I yelled. She spun around, shocked. "I'm not anybody else but me. Me, me, me! Summer Smith. And if you don't like it, it's just too bad."

I hadn't meant to cry, but I was starting, so I did a quick disappearing act up the stairs to my room. Mother made no attempt to stop me. I didn't cry long. Pretty soon, I was lying on my back in bed, thinking it all over. I had actually been fighting with Mother! Well, it wasn't the first time, but it was the first time I got everything said I intended to say. "I'm Summer Smith and if you don't like it, that's just too bad." I really liked that a lot. Me, the kid who ate barley casseroles to keep from upsetting anyone, was beginning to enjoy a good fight. Especially since I felt that I'd won it. Wow, I was changing so fast, I'd have to run full speed just to keep up with myself.

When Dad came home, he found Mother weeping in the living room and me still sprawled across my bed. But not weeping. He sat down on the edge of my bed, looking weary and forlorn.

"What's going on, Summer?"

"I don't know," I said. I couldn't exactly sum it all up in twenty-five words or less.

"Is it really all about returning a pair of shoes?"

"I don't think so."

"Neither do I. Well, what about the Whitman boy?"

I swallowed hard. "Dad, I told you both long ago, he has a girl friend, Cindy Grant. Ask anybody if you don't trust me."

"Of course I trust you."

"Mother doesn't."

"Don't be ridiculous."

"I'm not. She doesn't even trust me to wear those shoes I bought, let alone deal with Rod Whitman in a sensible manner."

Did I notice a smirk pass over Dad's face? Did he think I was being cute? I decided to ignore it.

"Summer," he said, "I have been thrown into the role of referee between you and your mother. I have to dash back and forth making judgments about who is 35 percent right and who is 65 percent wrong. And it's not fun."

"I guess not."

"I can't take sides. You're my daughter, but your mother is my wife. I can't play favorites, can I?"

"No."

"So, here's my position. Although I may not always show it, I love you very much. Do you know that?"

"Yes."

"And your mother loves you, too."

"I'm not so sure about that," I mumbled.

"What?"

"I said I'm not so sure about that. Even Reggie thinks that if it had been legal back then, I would have been an abortion."

Dad's mouth formed a little *o* and his eyes were two big *o*'s as well. It took him a couple of seconds before he could say anything.

"Where in the world did you get that idea, you and Reggie?"

"Well, look at Mother's scrapbooks. They're full of

pictures of Douglas, but there's not one of me. And look at how old she was when I was born. And how she looks at me sometimes, as if I were a creature from outer space, an *intruder*. It all adds up to one thing: I was a big, fat mistake."

Dad took out his pipe, looked around the room for an ashtray, then remembered where he was and took to biting on the pipe stem instead of smoking.

"Summer, there are things you don't know about your mother, things we saw no reason to tell you, and things we—well, I, for one—find it difficult to discuss with a young girl. However, perhaps the time has come. The truth is, we very much wanted you, your mother and I. The reason you came along so late in our lives is that there were two miscarriages between your brother's birth and yours. That's how badly your mother wanted you, Summer. Enough to risk the pain and grief of still another miscarriage."

My cheeks burned with shame, even though there was no way I could have known the truth. "Then why does she act as if I was—I don't know—as if she can't figure out what to do with me?"

Dad sighed and thought that over. "Well, it may be that she *doesn't* know exactly what to do with you. You know, all her life has been spent competing against other women. And winning. And here you are, a woman she can't beat."

"What do you mean? We've never even been in the same race."

"Oh, yes, you have. Same race as the rest of us. You

168

see, Summer, you have your entire life ahead of you. You have a future."

"Oh," I said, suddenly understanding. "And Mother's life is all behind her."

"That's the way she feels about it, right now. It's not true, of course. As long as you live, you have a future. But at this moment in her life, Mother isn't seeing things too clearly. I think with time and our support, though, she'll come around."

I was dying to ask if Mother was going through menopause, but you just don't ask your dad a question like that. Besides, I was pretty sure I knew the answer.

"I'll try my best, Dad. I really will."

"I know. And we'll try our best with you, too."

"Thank you," I said, quietly. Then, something occurred to me. "Does that mean I can keep my Casual Walking Shoes?"

Dad laughed. "I think that can be arranged. I'll talk it over with Mother."

"Whoopee!" I yelped, and wrapped myself around his neck for the most grateful hug in Middletown.

Dad asked for fifteen minutes alone with Mother, which I was all too happy to grant. Then I came downstairs. She was sitting on the sofa, very erect, watching me carefully. I knew I had to apologize first.

"Mother," I began. I had to clear my throat and start again. I was more nervous apologizing than I'd been fighting! "Mother, I'm sorry I said mean things to you. The soup was not really that bad."

"I'm sorry, too, Summer," she said, her mouth twitching as she spoke. "But the soup was horrible." Suddenly, Mother was laughing her bigger-than-all-outdoors laugh. Dad and I were swept right up in it.

I'd like to say we lived happily ever after, but we didn't. Not exactly. We fought and made up and fought and made up again and again. But it was okay. It didn't kill us.

# 20

Apparently Rod's invitation to the Sweetheart Dance didn't take right away. For quite a while, Cindy continued to sail away from him, guarded by her cluster of friends. I don't think General Grant enjoyed General Lee's surrender half as much, or dragged it out nearly as long. But she finally let Rod back into the winner's circle, back onto that golden throne by her side. One Monday morning, they passed me holding hands, and neither of them so much as flickered an eyelid in my direction. Cindy's ladies in waiting did, though, with many a smirk and uplifted eyebrow. If they thought they were going to humble me

171

the way they had Rod, they had another thought coming. By the third time the Royal Court swept past me, I was ready for them. The ladies giggled together, then shot me their best haughty glares. And I smiled cheerfully and gave them a slow, suggestive wink. Oh, I wish you could have been there to see their reaction. Mouths flew open, eyes darted back and forth. What could that Summer Smith possibly have to smile and wink about? To be perfectly frank, nothing. But *they* didn't know that. For a long time afterward, they lowered their heads respectfully when they saw me coming.

Soon after the Magic Wink, I looked up from a plate of truly disgusting chow mein (ptomaine) at lunch one day to find Reggie peering at me from the next table. It kind of shook me up. It must have done the same to her because she looked away quickly when our eyes met. I was dumping my milk carton in the trash when she came up beside me.

"Summer?" she said.

"Yes?"

"Um . . . can we talk?"

"*I* never stopped."

Nothing else was said until after we'd stacked our dishes and trays.

"You weren't really dating him, were you?" Reggie asked very quietly.

"No. Not really."

"But everybody said he kissed you on New Year's Eve."

"Reggie, *everybody* kisses *everybody* on New Year's Eve. Cowboys kiss their horses, witches kiss their cats.

Murray Hamm probably kissed Marjory Warren."

"Yech," Reggie said, pretending to shudder. "What was it like?" she asked, suddenly grinning.

"Murray kissing Marjory? I didn't see it."

"You know what I mean."

"Oh, *that*. Well, actually, I've been dying to tell you," I said. And arms linked, we giggled our way down the hall while I did. Reggie listened in a state of total rapture, which I was glad to see. I was afraid she might cry.

"Don't you love him anymore?" I wondered.

"I don't know," Reggie said, giving it a moment's serious thought. "When is Douglas coming home from California?"